The Walled Garden

for Geraldine

The Walled Garden

Michael Dean

Published by Black Moss Press
2450 Byng Road, Windsor, Ontario
N8W 3E8.
Black Moss books are distributed in Canada
and the United States by
Firefly Books Ltd. 250 Sparks Avenue,
Willowdale, Ontario, M2H 2S4.
All orders should be directed there.

This book was published with the financial assistance of
The Ontario Arts Council and The Canada Council.

Cover design by Kristina Russelo
Layout and Page Design by Kristina Russelo

Printed and bound in Canada by Hignell Printing, Ltd.,
Winnipeg, Manitoba.

CANADIAN CATALOGUING IN PUBLICATION DATA

Dean, Michael (Michael D.)
The walled garden

ISBN 0-88753-270-5

I. Title

PS8557.E2258W35 1993   C813'.54   C93-090365-X
PR9199.3.D43W35 1993

The author wishes to gratefully acknowledge the assistance of both
the Canada Council and the Ontario Arts Council in
providing grants in support of this book.

Book One

INTRODUCTION 1
(Life Inside the Garden)

> "Black Spot on roses is a very serious problem."
> *The Impatient Gardener,* Jerry Baker.

Eden

It all began in the walled garden. It began as I knelt barefoot in the earth with my axe raised high above my head and all my attention focused at the furthest extension of my arms where my hands gripped the axe handle. It began in the moment of pause when the axe reached the furthest extension of my arms and I was completely still for that brief moment, (as still as a figure from a 14th Century Italian fresco, likely a saint or an apostle in a baptistry painting from a cathedral like the one at Spoleto, or a mural from one of the monasteries at Siena or Florence or Assisi). Then the moment of pause ended, and I brought the axe down decisively, three times, into the hole in the earth and cut the last of the roots of the rosebush.

It all began in that brief moment of pause when the axe reached the furthest extension of my arms above my head. It began in that moment of pause on the afternoon of July 23, 1980 in the walled garden in the backyard of my house in Toronto, Canada. It ended three months later in the same garden on the evening of October 30, 1980. It began in the garden and ended in the Fall.

I did some research on the history of the pose I was making in that brief moment of pause, with my hands held together and my arms reaching high above my head, and found that in the Eastern spiritual tradition this gesture is known as *The Sign of Exultation,* (or *The Sign of Gold*), and that in the Western tradition it is known as *The Sign of Despair.* It took me three months to fully accept that I was making my pose in the Western tradition. You see, bringing down the axe and cutting the last of the roots of the rosebush was the event that caused the end of my ten year marriage to Claudette.

I was able to trace the Western roots of my gesture all the way back to Ancient Egypt. The first figure who ever made my pose was one of the two guards at the gates of the Underworld in a 5th Century B.C. Theban tomb sculpture. The most numerous examples of my gesture were made in the Italian Renaissance of the 14th and 15th Century. This was also the time when my gesture became known as the *Sign of Despair* through its association with figures of "the damned" in scenes of *The Last Judgement.* Other excellent examples appear in paintings of *The Last Judgement* and *The Expulsion from Paradise.*

Claudette and I disagreed seriously about which figure from Art History I resembled most. She did not think that I looked exactly like the Theban guard to the Underworld, (who was likely the god Anubis himself, the earliest Egyptian god of the dead), but thought I resembled one of the attending figures in Piombo's *The Last Judgement*, (Venice, 16th Century).

Claudette was right. And I was right. You see, it turned out that when I clasped my hands together and raised my arms high above my head, I was performing the first act in an ancient ritual of both death and resurrection. I was drawn to the death aspect, and Claudette was drawn to the resurrection aspect. However, the full significance of the removal of the rosebush from the garden can only be appreciated when we look at the gesture that Claudette was making while I was making mine. When we see both gestures we see the tableau that we were creating together, and by seeing this tableau we understand the significance of having a hole at the centre of our marriage where a rose used to be. *Thornless Rose?*

I was very much in love with Claudette when our marriage ended, and we both loved our roses. The rose was our central metaphor. All the elements of our marriage were formed in a centripetal structure around it. The rose is also the central metaphor of this novel. Specifically, the novel's central metaphor is not the rose itself, but *The Lady of the Rose*. *The Lady of the Rose* is the name I gave to the Lady who came out of the Earth, and into the garden, through the hole in the ground where the rosebush used to be.

The Introduction can be seen as a frame around that hole. The Introduction is a frame around the central metaphor of the novel. The Introduction is the wall around the garden containing the limits of my encounters with the Lady of the Rose, who was first known to me as *The Lady of the Rosebush*, (or *The Lady of the Rosetree*), and then finally as *The Lady who Plays the Rosegarden Game*. You may know her already as *The Lady Pierced in the Heart by Thorns*. The Introduction is the stone wall I have built to contain my experience of her.

Essentially then, the Introduction can be taken as the construction of the margin around the text. The Lady of the Rose is the central metaphor within the text.

The Introduction describes what takes place inside the garden when the point of observation is someplace on the garden wall. When the action of the novel is observed from the garden wall it can be seen as a tableau in a particular fresco, icon, or painting, in Art history.

The first time Claudette and I slept together was on the eve 'of All Saints Day, October 31, 1970. Then Claudette and I separated on October 30, 1980, the day before our tenth anniversary.

'Eve' of our tenth anniversary.

We were together ten years less one day. The only time I worked in the garden was when I dug out the rosebush. The house is my house, but the garden was always hers.

The wall around the garden is made of the same stone as the foundation of the house. Is the wall part of the garden or part of the house?

I am standing on the garden wall now. I am standing at the left-hand corner of the garden where the stone wall meets the house. I am on the perimeter. I am on the margin of the text. I am walking around and around (and around) the tableau that Claudette and I created in the walled garden of my backyard. I am looking for the perspective that will give everything its perfect symmetry. We will understand the true meaning of the removal of the rosebush from the garden only when we stand at the right place on the garden wall. Where I am now, at the left-hand corner of the stone wall where the wall meets the house, I can see myself kneeling in the garden with the axe raised above my head to the furthest extension of my arms, and I can see Claudette standing on the back porch under the arched trellis watching me. She is resting the side of her head on one hand while supporting the elbow of that arm with the other hand, the arm of which crosses her body at the abdomen.

Claudette's gesture is as ancient as the one I am making with my arms raised over my head. An excellent example of Claudette's pose can be found in the 13th Century Italian wood carvings of the figures of both The Virgin Mary and St. John the Apostle as they flank the figure of Christ in the sculptural tableau of *The Crucifixion*, (now at The Metropolitan Museum Cloister in New York). This gesture is known as the *Sign of Regret*, and is usually associated with crucifixion scenes or those of The Last Judgement. These themes of 'regret' and 'judgement' seem to support very nicely the themes of 'death' and 'resurrection' that we were discussing earlier when we were considering my gesture alone.

However, if we move around the perimeter of the text and examine the tableau from yet another place on the wall, (from the far right-hand corner where the wall is covered with the vines of the Virginia creeper), we can see that the tableau has distinct similarities to a 16th Century Persian garden painting. In fact, it resembles quite closely an illustration to the text of *Babur-Nama*, the autobiography of the Persian ruler who built the famous garden *Bagh-i Wafa* at Kabul. The figures corresponding to Claudette and me could be those of the two lovers meeting in the private enclosure at the centre of the garden.

This image of two lovers meeting in a Persian garden seems to contradict utterly the theme of death and resurrection that we were discussing earlier, until we accept that by observing the tableau from this place on the wall, (from the far right-hand corner covered with Virginia creeper), we are seeing the secret meaning of the removal of the rose-bush from the garden. By knowing the secret meaning we know the *out-come* of the death and resurrection of our marriage.

Let me be more specific and tell you what I learned when I saw the secret meaning: when the central metaphor of the rose was removed from our marriage, I learned that the hole left in the garden became an opening, or tunnel, that allowed Claudette and me to move freely back and forth between our garden in Toronto, Canada, and the private lover's enclosure at the centre of a royal Persian garden.

This comes as no surprise:

The garden in my backyard is a large rectangle shaped by the stone wall surrounding it. It is divided length-wise by a central path, then sub-divided into twelve equal parts by narrower paths in the short direc-tion. When it is seen from the ridge-line at the top of the house, or more exactly, from a theoretical point even higher than that, the garden resem-bles the pattern of a Persian carpet, in particular, a Persian carpet from Iran woven in the style of the Tabriz area.

What will become clear later, (in Introduction 2), is that the hole in the ground in our walled garden allowed Claudette and me to have free movement not only into royal Persian gardens, but into all the great gardens of the world. A great garden, for the purpose of this novel, is one that is filled with a deep calm, and a profound stillness. So, in this novel, the great gardens of the world are not necessarily the most famous ones, (like *The Alhambra* at Granada in Spain, or *The Hanging Gardens* of Babylon), but they can be obscure gardens like the 17th Century *English Country Garden* tended by the Fursden family near the village of Cadbury in the County of Devonshire, or the unknown garden in Konya, Turkey where the 13th Century Persian poet Rumi sat down and wrote the line, "I planted roses, but without you they were thorns".

I will tell you now what it was like when the deep calm and the profound stillness of all these great gardens came rushing into our walled backyard through the hole in the ground left by the rosebush. I will describe this from the same place on the garden wall:

I see myself placing the axe on the ground. I have just finished cutting the last of the roots of the rosebush. Now I put my hands into the hole in the ground and lift the knot of rosebush root from underneath, elevating it like a sacrament or like something taken from the chest of the body during surgery. I hold it suspended in my hands toward the sky.

I am now in the exact same posture that I was in when the novel began, except that I am holding the knot of rosebush root instead of the axe. You can see how easily everything falls into perspective when we look at the tableau from here, from the far right-hand corner of the garden wall.

This is the moment when the profound stillness of all the great gardens of the world come rushing into our back yard all at once. In summer, this is the kind of moment the insects occupy. (The shade doesn't move, the sprinkler seems to stop, you see wasps crawling on ripe things that have fallen from someplace higher up.)

Claudette is reaching out and taking hold of the stillness. She does this by not moving, by holding utterly to her performance of the ancient mantric sign of *Regret*.

Flies are not buzzing before her eyes in sunlight, and clouds of insects are not swarming near her mouth and eyes making her blink or turn away and lose the moment or transform it into one of listening instead of watching; which is what she seems to intend, to watch like this and to remember the stillness in its own image.

This is the moment when our marriage came to an end. It is clear to me that this is the moment when everything stopped between Claudette and me.

Normally things do not end like this in the middle of July, so early in the narrative before the rose-of-sharon is in bloom, long before the leaves have begun to change colour on the white maple and the linden. But this is the time when you begin to recognize that there is a pattern to everything, and that when the pattern is complete, things end.

In this case the pattern is a visual one, an image in clear air, unobscured and simple to hold.

I really admire the way Claudette holds the pattern, the way she holds the great stillness of this moment.

She holds the colour of the sky, which, when looking up at it now from the wall of the garden, looks exactly the same colour blue as the blue of the cloak worn by Our Lady in the 15th Century wood sculpture of *The Madonna of Perugia*, (Madonna with child, Perugia, Italy); and she holds the motion of the branches of the white oak over hanging the stone wall from the neighbour's yard; and she holds the intricate jumble of the virginia creeper covering the garden wall in the far right-hand corner, the corner with the lilacs and the russian olive tree.

I admire the way she holds all these things at once, and how she holds the garden in its wholeness, as if observing it from a theoretical height above Persia.

This is the beginning of the new stillness I have come to know in Claudette.

Do you understand now?

This "new stillness in Claudette" is the same thing as "It all began in the walled garden", except seen from a different place on the margin. By standing on the garden wall I am also standing on the margin of the text, and from here I see that the "new stillness in Claudette" is what the first sentence of the novel looks like when seen from the back right-hand corner of the garden wall.

I see myself lowering the rosebush root to the earth, and the moment loses its stillness. The stillness is in Claudette entirely now. I look exhausted.

I see myself take a handkerchief from my right pant pocket, and at the same time I notice a coin drop out of the pocket and fall into the hole in the ground where the rosebush used to be. The coin is a 1939 English half-crown which had been my father's good luck charm when he was a fighter pilot with the RCAF in the Battle of Britain. It was the only thing of my father's that I still treasured. I see myself wipe my forehead with the handkerchief as I sit on the ground and reach into the hole to pick up the coin. Then I see myself stop, deciding to leave the coin in the hole where the rosebush used to be. I look into the hole for a long moment, then I take a handful of earth and drop it into the hole on top of the coin. Then I turn my head away and reach out and take hold of my right ankle with both hands and begin to examine my feet.

I've always been troubled by my feet. I considered them the most unattractive part of me. Claudette used to comment on this, especially in the beginning of our relationship, although she referred to them merely as "your poor vulnerable feet".

I am seated on the ground with my hands on my ankle, and Claudette is beside me suddenly, asking if I am all right. "What have you done to your poor vulnerable feet!"

"I have a thorn in my foot." I say.

"You're always doing something to those feet," she says. "Your toenails are like snail shells."

I remove the thorn from my foot and say: "I have just been initiated. Now these are gardener's feet." I reach out and place the thorn gently in Claudette's open hand.

"This is not a rose thorn," she says. "It comes from a laurel and there are no laurel trees or laurel hedges in this garden. Be sure to do something against infection."

I hold both my feet in both my hands and rock onto my back, raising my feet to heaven: "Oh Lord, heal these feet! Saint Phocas of Sinope, patron saint of all gardeners, pray for them against infection!"

"You're not funny!" Claudette says. "I don't want to hear about the saints anymore. I mean it. This is the end of all that. No more saints, no martyrs, no miracles. They don't mean anything anymore. It's over."

This is when I know it's over, that everything is over between us.

Claudette takes a step towards the house, then comes back and kicks the root knot of the rosebush and both bundles of rose branches. On each kick she yells, in french: "Maudit! Chalice! Tabernacle!"

You should understand something: each of the plots of the garden had been given a name, and each name was the name of a saint who had appeared in a painting while making a particularly interesting gesture or mantric sign. We understood these gestures as the saints' way of communicating with us.

You should not interpret this as something frivolous. You see, the saints protected and guided our marriage from the beginning. I think they even brought us together. In fact, we discovered our love for the saints on the first night we slept together. We discovered our love for each other on the second night.

You should view the twelve sections of the garden, (each one named for a saint), as the twelve sections, or chapters, of this novel.

The Introduction is a way of presenting the elements that appear in each of the sections. However, because this is a perennial garden, many of the elements cannot be confined to only one section, and appear throughout the novel, sometimes as weeds.

On our second night together, the night we discovered our love for each other, November 1, 1970, Claudette had said: "Something significant happened today. I received a sign from heaven about us. No, really! A sign from heaven. It was a sign of blessing on this union."

We had both laughed at this.

Nevertheless, for ten years, the saints looked after us. They looked down on us, as if from a little distance removed, as if from the top of a wall that surrounded and protected us.

That's how this novel is written. That's what the novel is about: I have learned to be with the saints on the wall, and they have learned to be with me in the garden.

I have written the novel from both places. You can learn to do this too. We are all saints digging at the roots of things, telling each other stories about life on our knees. We are all gardeners who can stand back at a place a little removed, and give each other blessing, for what we find in digging.

Introduction 2
(What the Saints Saw
From the Wall)

> The English Laurel,*laurocerasus*, is a
> member of the rose family, genus
> *rosaceae*.
> (*Taylor's Guide to Shrubs* p.385)

There is a large flowering shrubbery, a rose-of-sharon, at the back of the garden on the opposite wall to where I had been digging up the rosebush root in Introduction 1. The rose-of-sharon was not in bloom of course, (it does not bloom until mid-August), but something occurred next to it, in the same moment that I was elevating the rosebush root into the stillness: one of the saints came down from the wall and entered the garden.

He entered in an ecstasy.

He was not an authorized saint, but one of those with the title 'Venerable', still awaiting final elevation to sainthood. He was a 'venerable' mystic, an important member of the canon of saints who watched us from the top of the stone wall surrounding the garden. The mystics were those who watched us most closely. They have been keenly interested in the outcome of this novel.

Behind the mystics, just slightly further back on the margin, was another group of saints known as The Desert Fathers, a group of coptic monks who had lived together in community in the deserts of Egypt in the first four centuries of Christianity. This group included the European monk Saint Cassian. Cassian was not the saint who entered the garden in the still moment, but he had a strong influence on the saint who did. He too has had a great interest in the outcome of this novel.

Cassian was a European monk who travelled from Marseille to the deserts of Egypt in the year 419 to study the physical and mental exercises of the hermit communities of the Egyptian desert. His record of their methods of prayer and asceticism is known as Cassian's *Conferences*, and was used for several hundred years as the guideline for the emerging communities of European monks.

Seated and standing on the wall of the garden, ranked in tiers around us, row upon row in the margin, were all the saints of the Eastern and Western synaxories and martyrologies. They were all in distinctive gestures and poses, some with a hand placed on a forehead, or both hands crossed gently at the heart, or with one knee bent, or simply bowing from the waist. Among the saints were martyred virgins, (and martyrs who were not virgins); confessor saints from the later centuries; saints associated with specific places; patron saints of gardens and ships-under-sail; and patrons of learning, self-denial and the making of a good death.

The saint who entered the garden during the still moment was a mystic of the 17th Century, the Venerable Augustine Baker, (born 1575 in Wales, died 1641 in London, England). Augustine Baker looked magnificent as he entered the garden. A light was shining on his face from above, and his left arm was held so that it was bent at the elbow, and his right hand was out in front of his heart. He was one of the two saints who became intimate with us in the garden. The other saint was Marguerite Bourgeoys (born in 1620 in France, died in 1700 in Montreal, Canada).

Augustine Baker and Marguerite Bourgeoys walked with us in the garden, strolling among the growing things, among the things that throw shade, and the things that fall from trees and break open and swarm with crawling insects.

The function of the saints has always been to look on from the margin, and to evaluate the state of the garden, to reconcile contradictions within it, as within a narrative.

They function as metaphor.

Like metaphor.

Their place is a place of commentary.

When Augustine Baker joined us, he climbed into the garden beside the rose-of-sharon. He entered the garden in a state of ecstasy. He was a Benedictine monk on a secret mission to England. It was 1620, the time of the English Reformation, when being a Catholic priest was an act of treason against the crown punishable by death by beheading. He stood barefoot in the English country garden of the Fursden family, near the village of Cadbury in the county of Devonshire.

He was in an ecstasy. He later identified this experience as his 'third conversion' to the mystical way.

He walked barefoot into the garden and smelled the wild loose-strife and the blossoms of the moon-flower vine. He smelled the fruit of the blackberry bush. Insects buzzed before his eyes. The buzzing grew louder and louder until it made a cracking sound near him or inside him, and that's when he noticed the laurel hedge at the bottom of the yard. In front of the hedge he saw a woman standing, smiling in welcome. Roots like those of the laurel were growing downward from her feet. Her hair was wild. Her hair was the laurel in blossom.

Baker was halfway across the lawn. He saw that the woman was naked and that her body was beautiful, and that her nipples were roses, and that the bush between her legs was the blackberry bush. He tasted berries on his tongue, and smelled the smell of roses and laurel blossom.

He smelled the loam rising from himself.

Baker's body became fastened to its place. The light that had been shining in his face moved downward through his body into the earth. His skin became tree bark and his hair the branches of the linden. This moment was identical to the moment in which I elevated the rosebush root from its hole in the ground and Claudette reached out and took hold of the stillness.

Augustine Baker is best known as the man who renewed the mystical tradition in seventeenth century England. He recovered the works of earlier English mystical writers Richard Rolle, Julian of Norwich, and the anonymous author of *The Cloud of Unknowing*. His own visionary writings were collected under the title *Sancta Sophia*, (Holy Wisdom). In his writings he investigated the process of a contemplative life, insisting that a religious practice was meaningless without contemplation at the centre of it. Life was a centripetal structure. Everything fanned outward from a centre. The centre was contemplation. His primary reference was Cassian's *Conferences*.

In the still moment in the garden, (in the stillness held by the Lady of the Laurel Hedge), Augustine Baker grew closer to God. He uprooted himself from Earth and entered divine gravity.

He uprooted himself by rejecting the Lady of the Laurel Hedge, by forcing the temptation of Her nakedness from his mind, and by spurning Her as the work of the devil.

He entered divine gravity, and something in his lower legs gave way, as if his ankles snapped and disconnected him from the Earth.

Augustine Baker climbed down from the wall and stood behind me in the moment of stillness that entered our garden when I elevated the rosebush root from the earth and held it at the furthest extension of my arms toward the sky. This was the moment when our garden was joined to all the great gardens of the world. Augustine Baker came to me from the seventeenth century English country garden of the Fursden family in Devonshire, and the Lady of the Laurel Hedge came with him. In fact, Augustine Baker descended from the wall just after the Lady of the Laurel Hedge rose out of the hole in the ground. She brushed past me and went straight for Claudette. A thorn of the laurel stuck in my foot near the ankle.

Augustine Baker came to stand behind me just as I took a handkerchief out of my pocket and pulled my father's coin with it so that it fell into the hole in the ground. Augustine Baker spoke to me as we both watched the Lady of the Laurel Hedge dance to a place behind Claudette. "I have come to bring you a great blessing," he said to me. He pointed to the Lady of the Laurel Hedge: "I want you to deliver a message to her on my behalf. I want you to be the messenger between my world of divinity and the Lady's world of darkness. That is my blessing upon you. And when your work is complete, a disruption in both of us, occurring at the ankles, will be healed."

There was a reference to my relationship with Augustine Baker in Introduction I: "I've always been troubled by my feet. I considered them the most unattractive part of me."

It was a subtle reference.

Nevertheless, it is the hidden text of the entire novel. The novel is the story of what I learned while fulfilling the request of Augustine Baker. It is also the result of that learning, in that the structure of the novel is based on the pattern that the Lady and I wove in our successive meetings in the garden, (unaware of how beautifully we were working together, discovering this beauty only at the end when we turned around and beheld the final pattern), as if we had been the two threads of the jufti knot, the knot used in the weaving of Persian carpets.

Persian carpets are based on the pattern of enclosed Islamic gardens. Therefore, the novel is structured on the plan of a classic Islamic garden. The Introduction is the surrounding wall, and the twelve chapters are the twelve symmetrical plots.

Structurally the novel makes reference to another literary work, the twelfth century Sufi masterpiece *Gulistan*, (The Rose Garden), by Sadi, which is also structured, in its formal elements, on the pattern of a classic Islamic garden. The design of an Islamic garden is meant to express the beauty of Heaven on Earth, (not Heaven as a theoretical point above us at a place removed, but Heaven as the human heart transformed into a paradise because it is filled with the presence of the Beloved). The classic Islamic garden is the presence of the Beloved in the heart. It is built on the exact dimension and perfect symmetry of that heart.

The novel is about to begin. As it progresses, all the gardens of the novel will be superimposed on one another. This will form an immensely complicated pattern.

If we consider this pattern visually, it can only be duplicated in something as intricate as the design of a Persian carpet.

If we consider it as an experience of time, however, the same pattern can be re-created automatically, and in a manner which can be easily followed, in the left-to-right weaving of the text.

CHAPTER 1
(for St Phocas of Sinope,
patron saint of gardeners)

> "Garden roses have been grown in
> Canada since the time of the first
> convent garden in Quebec."
> *Roses for Canadian Gardens,*
> Roscoe A. Fillmore.

It is only from the margin around the text that we are allowed a place of commentary upon the narrative, like having a view from a wall looking inward.

We are inside the text now, looking out at ourselves as we also *out stand here * making sense of it all, observing what takes place in here, here inside the garden where the Venerable Augustine Baker denied his vision of the Lady in his Third Conversion, and by this , escaped the pull of mere gravity and entered divine gravity, snapping the roots that held him to Earth, becoming unlike the rest of us anymore, we gardeners, who kneel cutting rosebush roots, and add lime to the soil to kill the blight of the Black Spot fungus.

As I have mentioned already in Introduction 2, the other significant saint who participated intimately with us in the garden, is Marguerite Bourgeoys, who founded the Congregation of the Sisters of Notre Dame de Bon Secours in Montreal, and who died there in 1700.

There is a reason why I didn't show Marguerite Bourgeoys climbing down from the margin into the garden, along with Augustine Baker, in Introduction 2.

You see, she was in the garden all along. She was in the garden before it was built. In fact, she was the centrepiece and focal point of its design.

I find this a fascinating story. She entered the garden through Claudette. The rosebush that I had been digging out in the Introduction was grown from a cutting from Claudette's aunt's rosebush, in Rimouski Quebec, on the Gaspé. Her name was Huguette, Tante Huguette. She had been a nun of the Congregation of Notre Dame de Bon Secours, the order of nuns founded by Marguerite Bourgeoys in Montreal.

Tante Huguette's rosebush in Rimouski was planted by her in the summer of her death. She was generally considered a saint by her sisters, (Claudette's mother, and her mother's six sisters), due to the profound nature of Tante Huguette's death, at twenty-one, of consumption.

The Congregation of Notre Dame de Bon Secours is a teaching order of nuns, and Huguette - had she lived long enough to take her final vows - was to teach art.

During the last few weeks of her life she had completed a deeply devotional series of six paintings dedicated to the image of Our Lady: "Madonna and Child in the Rose Arbour", (a pastiche of Lochner's of the same name, 1450), "Our Lady of the Rose Tree," (likely based on a fourteenth Century Italian baptistry fresco), "The Lady in the Grove", (in the French style of the late Renaissance). The remaining three of the paintings were done with progressively broader strokes, until twigs and bits of fabric and dried flowers were added directly to the paint surface, in keeping with the folk-art style of the Gaspé.

Tante Huguette's rosebush in Rimouski was known to the family as Tante Huguette's rosebush, but when it bloomed, the flowers were called The Roses of Our Lady.

All the members of Claudette's family had a rosebush of their own started from Tante Huguette's. Claudette's cutting was sent to her by her mother six months after Claudette moved from Montreal to Toronto. It arrived in the mail, wrapped in moist tissue, on the morning following the night she slept with me for the first time.

This is the "sign from heaven" that Claudette told me about on our second night together. "It is a blessing directly from Tante Huguette in heaven." She had said.

The next morning Claudette had gone into the walled garden in my backyard and planted the rose cutting. She planted Tante Huguette's history, and the history of Europe, and the history of art and religion.

So, when the Black Spot fungus killed the rosebush ten years later, Claudette knew it was all over between us, and that a blessing from Tante Huguette, which had protected her from the moment of her birth, was lifted from her heart forever.

Claudette and I were deeply in love with all the saints. On the first night we made love, Claudette stroked the scar on my upper abdomen and said: "You're just like a saint. You have a wound on your chest like a martyr, a scruffy beard like a hermit, and the nose of an archangel. In fact your nose is the most saintly part of you. It's the nose of the Archangel Gabriel in *The Annunciation* by Fra Angelico that you showed us in class today."

I was deeply disappointed. I said: "I like to think I resemble a great monk of the late-monastic period. In fact, I like to think I resemble the last great monk of the monastic period, or someone like the earlier fourteenth Century author of "The Cloud of Unknowing". Of course, nobody knows who he was, but if they did, I know I would look like him. Besides, if they knew who he was, they would canonize him, the way they have the other visionaries, like Teresa of Avila, or Julian of Norwich."

"But Julian of Norwich was never canonized."

"She should have been." I said. " She did as much for the English language as Chaucer. She was his contemporary, and did her writing in Middle English as well. In a way, her contribution was even greater than Chaucer's, because she was using the colourful dialects and slang of Middle English to express something more difficult than what we find in Chaucer. She was expressing her ecstatic visions, which were entirely simple, yet universal and thoroughly personal."

"They don't canonize you for loving language."

"My point exactly."

Claudette laughed and touched my scar again. "Your scar, that's the same place they show the wound on Christ. You know, the one from the lance that killed him and nothing ran out but water."

I got up from the bed and went to the book case that holds my leather-bound books. Claudette came and stood beside me. "Listen to this," I said. "Listen to Dame Julian, anchoress, from the church of St. Julian, Conisford, Norwich, (1342-1416)."

> "God shewed me a little thing, the quantity of an hazel-nut, in the palm of my hand; and it was as round as a ball. I looked thereupon with eye of my understanding, and thought: What may this be? And it was answered generally thus: It is all that is made."

Beside the text, in the margin, there was an asterisk and a note in my own handwriting: "ref., the 'nut' like an individual bead of the rosary (should have been rosewood), rosary/ rosarium/ rosegarden".

"Look at that!" Claudette said, "Rosegarden. You wrote rosegarden!" She placed her finger on my marginal note, blocking my sight and disrupting my reading of Julian of Norwich before it began.[*]

"I did my thesis for my doctorate on the history of the rosary, as it evolved in Western Art from image of devotion to symbol of feminine divinity. Essentially - although this is not entirely accurate - it evolved from "the rose", the incorruptible rose of Persia."

---

[*] For the convenience of the reader, however, the text reference is shown here in its entirety.

I think that's when Claudette fell in love with me. Certainly, that's when she started telling me all her secrets about Tante Huguette. I know that's when she decided to begin her garden in my walled backyard, and that the garden had to begin with Tante Huguette.

Following is the story that Claudette told me on that night, our second night together in the Fall of 1970. In it you will see for yourself the emerging metaphor of this novel, which, like all metaphors in continuous prose, creates a central image which binds the elements together in a centripetal configuration around it.

"When I was seven years old, on the day before my First Communion, my mother took me to the Church of Notre Dame de Bon Secours in Old Montreal, where Tante Huguette, my mother's eldest sister, had been a nun. She showed me the altar where the nuns have a wax mannequin dressed in the habit of a nun of the seventeenth century. The nun is lying 'in-state', behind glass in the side altar. It's meant to be Marguerite Bourgeoys, the founder of the Order. But on that day, and for many years after, I believed it was Tante Huguette.

"On the way home, we drove past L'Hotel Dieu, the old hospital at the foot of Mount Royal, and my mother made the sign of the cross and nudged me to do the same, and said, 'That's where Huguette died'.

"I'm even named for her, and I've prayed to her all my life and she's protected me." I said,

"How can you be named for Huguette when you don't have the same name?"

"Her ordination name was Marie-Claudette. When I was baptized that was the name I was given: Marie-Claudette."

"Your life was very complicated before you were born."

"No, it was sad. You see, after Huguette became a nun she came home to the Gaspé, from Montreal, for her mother's funeral. You see, Huguette's mother, my own mother's mother, had left so many small children behind, (there were ten children altogether, and my mother was the third youngest and she was only two-and-a-half. Imagine!), well, because of the young ones, Huguette sacrificed herself and stayed home to care for them. Until the consumption happened, when she went back to Montreal to make a good death and do the paintings.

"But she left the rosebush 'for all of us small children to remember her by, and to remind us she will always take care of us even from heaven'."

I said, "You've got that memorized!"

"Oh yes." She said. "In French and English."

Then, the next morning, Claudette planted Tante Huguette's rosebush. Then, ten years later, the rosebush died.

It died like a word mistaken for a metaphor which, when asked to carry more than it could, or cared to, was dropped altogether from the text.

Or, it died as if something in it snapped, like the feet of a gardener unable to root the heart of a saint to Earth. [1]

---

[1] Note how the second metaphor demonstrates the first, but how the two help explain something of the other. [2]

[2] Which is often the case when the same thing is seen from two distinct places on the continuous wall surrounding it.

1st Purport [*] :
Explication de texte

Metaphor is the centripetal structure within continuous prose that serves the text in the same way that the knot serves weaving.

Metaphor is to text

as

knot is to textile.

The carpets of Islam were designed on the patterns of enclosed gardens. These gardens were designed to reflect the paradise of the Beloved. These paradise gardens were physical expressions of the Beloved's presence in the human heart.

Metaphor then is a knot in the heart, one beat in the experience of its continuous beating.

These knots, when repeated in a left-to-right sequence, create a pattern. But, because each knot is also a moment, weaving becomes a way of repeating the finite moment, infinitely.

The infinite is captured in the finite in the pattern of the weave, in the symbol of visual unity the weaving creates in the finished carpet design.

Of course, the same is true of continuous prose in the novel.

Unique to the novel, however, is the ability to reconcile all apparent discrepancies within the text, by using the intermediate sentence, or chapter. Like this one.

So, as we turn each page, we move no closer to infinity. But each page is attached to the preceding page, and altogether these pages create a pattern that, when taken as a whole in the finished book, become a symbol of the infinite.

How we love to hold a book. We hold it in one hand and turn the pages, one at a time, with the fingers of the other hand. How we love to turn pages, and to repeat this turning endlessly, as an acceptance of our limit, as a form of reconciliation with the infinite, which has caused such grief in us because we cannot hold it except in the heart, except in one moment at a time, squeezing paradise with each heart beat, running our fingers down the edges of paper as we pause, then turn the page, then pause again, then continue turning, as if we have done this forever, and can keep on doing this forever.

---

[*] Purport: the meaning, sense, or tenor of a text or document.

CHAPTER 2:
For Sadi
(1194-1291)

> "Each word of Sadi has seventy-two
> meanings." (Introduction to *Gulistan*,
> Indries Shah.)

With this novel I have undertaken the task of replacing the central metaphor in a piece of continuous prose, and of finding a new image that will bind the elements together in a centripetal configuration around it. The end of my marriage is the event I am using to illustrate this process.

The symbol of the rose is gone from the novel, and the rosebush itself is gone from the garden. In their place is an emptiness, and a hole in the ground. 'Emptiness' is also the name I gave to the phase of my life that began when the rosebush died. The emptiness lasted one year. During that time Claudette left me, and the shadow of the hole where Tante Huguette's rosebush used to be, grew darker and darker.

First, the shadow of the hole spread to the thickening shade of the linden, and then to the thin shadow of branches cast in shade. It spread to the darkness of wet lawn after night rain, and to the stiff lupin stocks bent by that rain. It moved onto the branches that were blown down in the night, and it crawled with things that move in dew.

The shadow of the rosebush was not a blooming and a ripening. It was not a flourishing of leaves and of maple seeds that swirl downward on a breeze. It was not late-summer blossoms or the fruit of trees. It was a shadow cast on a bedroom window blind. It nodded back and forth at night. It moved thickly and was pendulous.

The shadow overtook me in the garden in early October as I was picking up the fallen branches after the night rain and Claudette was watching me through the kitchen window.

Claudette wasn't laughing at my jokes anymore. In fact, she had stopped laughing entirely weeks earlier when she carried the shadow of the hole into the house. The shadow followed Claudette right into the bedroom. It followed her right into her dreams. The shadow attached itself to Claudette and became a dream figure of a woman who repeated a name over and over in Claudette's mind. Then the shadow woman started wandering throughout the house, following Claudette from room to room all day long.

The woman was dressed in black, and she always stood before a window looking out into the garden, or she reached for the window, opened it slowly, then looked out. She stood there repeating the same name, or phrase, over and over in Claudette's mind.

Claudette had not seen the woman's face yet, but she recognized her each time by her sorrow. She knew, of course, that it was Tante Huguette. And she knew that Tante Huguette had been renewed in some way and was bearing a message to her from heaven.

None of this was a problem for Claudette. She felt that the transformation occurring in our marriage was a reflection of a greater transformation occurring in heaven. She knew that Tante Huguette had changed in some way, (the change having been signalled by the death of the rosebush), and that, likely, this transformation indicated a shift in Huguette's position in heaven to one closer to God. Or else it meant that heaven had altered itself from within and had caused the shift in Tante Huguette. This shift had caused a corresponding shift in Claudette's relationship to God, which she needed badly to understand.

Claudette lost interest in the garden completely. She had spent all her life in gardens, having been told by her mother that she had inherited Tante Huguette's love of roses. But even giving up gardening was not a problem for her.

What was a problem for Claudette was the realization that she herself had begun standing before windows and staring out, losing track of time, listening to her heart beating, listening and listening until she had isolated her attention on one single beat, until that beat had become all there was, and time didn't exist, and her heart had become the large heart of all women who suffer.

On the morning in early October, (when I picked up the branches blown down in the night rain, and Claudette watched me from the kitchen window), I told Claudette that I didn't like what was happening to her, and that I didn't like The Lady in Black. Claudette startled both of us with the degree of her anger over this. Then she said that my charming idiosyncrasies had become annoying habits, and that my 'mind work' (the art reviews and criticism) was nothing but cold manipulations of other people's creative energy and heart. "You ask passionate questions then give intellectual answers," she said.

We had this argument in early autumn, when the daylilies were blooming and the purple loosestrife was tied upright again after the night rain, and the shaded astilbes were behind the daylilies, and the night-scented nicotania was high under the bedroom window. By then, by early autumn, nothing was the same anymore between Claudette and me, and by late autumn she moved out.

By uprooting the rosebush, Claudette and I had begun our journey into the hole at the centre of the garden, the hole at the centre of ourselves where the compelling metaphor should have been located.

I am an expert on metaphors. I use them all the time in my work. I saw the problem of our marriage very simply, and this is how I explained it to Claudette that afternoon:

"The metaphor at the centre of our marriage is gone. If this metaphor can be seen spatially, (which is how you must see it, because you're an artist), it would be like the design at the centre of a hand-woven Persian carpet. This centre must hold the tension of the entire work by drawing the disparate elements of the visual field into an overall unity. For a focal point of this intensity, you can only imagine something at the centre as perfect as the rose. Well, now that the rose is gone you feel that everything is gone and that there is nothing left of the marriage until you can find the new centre.

"But if we consider this same Persian carpet from the perspective of the writer, (from my perspective), we can see that the pattern of the carpet is more the result of the progressive left-to-right movement of the weaving process. From this perspective the perfect centre becomes simply another moment in the act of weaving, gaining significance only later, when I can look back and behold the finished work all at once. For me, the new centre of our marriage is something we will discover in our day-to-day life together."

This is when Claudette exploded and accused me of giving intellectual answers to passionate questions. But frankly, I still think I was right about why Claudette and I were at an impasse: she saw the perfect rose at the centre of our marriage simply as something visual, and I was aware of it as pure process. Where I *did* go wrong was not appreciating how, for Claudette, the centre had shifted, and the perfect rose was no longer at the centre of our marriage, but was at the centre of her own life. The centre of her world had shifted, and she saw the rose inside herself suddenly and with clarity, and she had never seen anything so beautiful. I was experiencing the centre of myself merely as something that was created in the repetitive activity of my daily life, an activity like weaving which resembles writing.

In fact, I can say now that there was nothing beautiful in the pattern I was weaving at that time in my daily life. There was something missing from the weave. I wasn't ready to bind the edges and roll it out in a public place where other people could walk around and around (and around) it, admiring the tightness of the knots and the evenness of the weave, asking me questions like: "How did you remove the rose from the centre of your marriage and still manage to include it in the overall pattern of your life?" Well , this is my secret: I learned to add thin strands of rose shadow to the weave. Even the rose has a shadow.

Claudette and I were in our bedroom after packing the last of her things. We were watching the shadow of the linden on the window-blind. It was bending slowly in the night storm.

I said: "It is thick and pendulous."

She said: "It looks like I feel, like the thing that's moving in me."

Branches were blowing down in the wind. The grass was littered with them in the morning, littered with crawling things that move in dew.

Chapter 3
(For Saint Cassian)

> "...through continual repetition
> an evocative verse usually
> remains evocative."
> Cassian, *Conferences*.

Every page of this novel has the same structure as the walled garden behind my house. All the events of the novel can be seen as occurring at various points on the central path as you walk toward the shaded grove and pass in and out of the patches of sunlight under the linden tree where insects light on blossoms. I write the novel on the love seat in the shaded grove, with this pen, on vellum.

Writing is the pattern of sunlight and shadow on the page.

Reading is the motion of the shadow in a breeze.

I draw an overhead plan of my walled garden, then write the names of blossoming plants and trees: climbing hydrangea, Russian olive, the fragrant cloud: a rose.

The shade moves back and forth on a breeze.

I read: foxglove and iris, hollyhock, columbine and larch.

This garden is a writer's garden. It is a descendant of the Garden of Eden, which was the first garden created by a writer.[1]

The walls around Eden were a late addition to the garden. They were built in the 1st Century A.D. by Philo of Alexandria. Philo (20 B.C. - 35 A.D.) was an Alexandrian Jew and a Hellenic philosopher. He built walls around Eden by applying the logical system of Aristotle to an analysis of the Bible.

Philo, like the other Hellenic Jews of Alexandria, felt that he must "reconcile Juadaism with the culture of the Western world".[2] As a Jew he wanted to honour his belief that the Bible was divinely inspired, that it was itself the word of God, while as a Hellenic scholar he felt bound to demonstrate that the teachings of the Bible coincided with the impersonal doctrines of the Greeks. This was the beginning of textual interpretation.This was the building of the wall that gained an overview of paradise. Philo brought perspective to the Garden of Eden by inter-

---

[1] "The Bible...beginning with the story of Eden...was originally written with black fire on white fire."
Moses ben Naman, ref. *Kabbalah*, Gershom G. Scholem.

[2] Biggs, *The Christian Platonists of Alexandria*.

preting the Bible from an outside source. He began his commentary by claiming that the story of Genesis was an allegory, and that Eden was not an actual garden, but was an analog for the soul. That's how he built the wall around Eden and gave the garden perspective.

He built the wall by analogy.

Philo opened the Bible to commentary from a Hellenic perspective and, by this, developed the foundation for allegorical language. He created a new image of God by taking the Greek idea that there is an impersonal concept called Logos (Cosmic Reason) which gives order and intelligibility to the world, and combined this with the Hebrew belief that God is literal and speaks personally to his people in the Bible. Philo placed language on an analogic footing, and gave it a "deeper meaning". In other words, the Bible remained the word of God, but now it had to be read on two levels: "...the literal sense is the body, while the soul is the secret sense underlying the written word." [Philo, *De Vita Contemplativa*]. In the end this made God into the secret meaning in every text, and made Him the ultimate metaphor that everything must be like in some way.

Hebrew scholars have always said that the Bible must be read on two levels - the level of commentary upon the literal text being the *midrash*. Philo simply replaced traditional rabbinic midrash with a new Hellenic midrash. In the end, his commentaries "... transformed the good Father and Lord of the Bible into the Eternal Negation of [Greek] dialectics".[3] His commentaries also opened the way for the Christian Fathers of Alexandria, Clement & Origen, to identify the impersonal principle of Logos as Christ.[4]

Philo helped change language, and the change started with a commentary on the garden of Eden. Since then all writing in Western culture has been garden writing.

Garden writing has appeared in two forms in the West: there is the journal writing of the gardener, and the commentary writing of the landscape architect. The gardener sees everything from inside the garden, and the landscape architect sees it all from the top of the garden wall. The gardener is literal and the landscape architect finds the meaning. In terms of this novel, the gardener tells the story of what happened

---

[3] *History of Christianity*, The First Three Centuries, Vol. 1, Mosheim.

[4] "Just as the Alexandrian Jews had allegorized the Old Testament, so the Apostolic Fathers...allegorized it in order to make a witness for Christian Truth." *The Seventeenth Century Background*, Basil Willey.

to me and Claudette in the garden, and the landscape architect writes the Purports about the story.

Language requires belief. Philo changed writing forever when he demonstrated that language is, in fact, a belief-system unto itself. Metaphor encloses it. Metaphor is a wall around the garden of Eden.

Before Claudette came to live here there was nothing in my back yard except ragged lawn and some creeping ground cover in the corners. I used to hate gardening - even cutting the grass.

Then Claudette planted Tante Huguette's rosebush and started the climbing hydrangea. Immediately I insisted that we make a plan for the garden. Claudette chose the trees and shrubs, and she planted all the flowers. I designed the shape of the beds. This created a problem for me right away: whenever I entered the garden I could only see the plan I had made, I could not see the wild and unpredictable quality of the things growing around me. I told Claudette: "I am blinded by the order under-lying and informing these growing things." Claudette understood: this tendency in me had always been a weakness in our marriage. This same tendency is the weakness at the heart of allegorical language: there is an assumption that the most real thing is something abstract, while the image or personification is created for the sake of the abstraction.

Just as I wrote that line, (in fact, just as I wrote the word "abstraction"), a mysterious breeze blew into the garden, and as a result, the patches of sunlight began moving rapidly back and forth across the page. This forced me to stop writing. I rested my head against the back of the love seat and looked up and saw the sky through the branches of the linden and felt the breeze on my cheek. I'm not sure, but I think I fell asleep for a moment. I remember closing my eyes, and I remember the breeze dying down, and I remember sitting up again and looking over my notes and coming to the last sentence that I'd written earlier, and coming to the word "abstraction", and wondering: if language requires belief, then what is reading: a form of religious practice, or faith, or patience, or a breeze in paradise?

2nd Purport:
Translating Philo

> "...the literal sense is the body, while
> the soul is the secret sense underlying
> the written word."
> *Philo.*

The rosebush that I removed from the walled garden behind my house was started from a cutting taken from the rosebush that Tante Huguette planted in Rimouski in the summer of her death. The Rimouski rosebush was started by Tante Huguette from a cutting she took from a rosebush in the convent garden of the Sisters of Notre-Dame-de-Bon-Secours, in their Mother House on Rue Saint-Jean-Baptiste in old Montreal.

Claudette told me two contradictory stories about the origin of that convent rosebush. Both stories were told to Claudette by her mother. In one story the convent rosebush in Montreal came from a cutting from a rosebush in Quebec City, from the first convent garden that successfully transplanted a European hybrid rose in Canada. In the other story the convent rosebush came directly to Montreal from France in the seventeenth Century, brought by Marguerite Bourgeoys herself on the same voyage of 1672 when she brought to Canada the famous miraculous statuette of the Madonna, which she had received as a gift from her benefactor Baron de Fancamp.

If the first story is true, then the rosebush in my backyard is the descendant of the very first rose that ever bloomed in Canada. If the second story is true then the rosebush, through association with the miraculous statuette of the madonna, could be said to be, itself, miraculous.

Nevertheless, the rosebush is a metaphor.

In its literal, or obvious, sense the rosebush is either a metaphor for the regenerating capacity of life that gives us continuity, (if the rosebush came from Quebec City), or it is a metaphor for the transcendent, miraculous energy that injects itself into the continuum, (if it came to Canada on the same voyage with the miraculous statuette of the madonna).

In its secret sense the rosebush resolves these two contradictory ideas; that is, in its secret sense the rosebush represents the love we hold in us that survives all conditions, *so that* we can receive the love that enters us miraculously from outside, love that is freely-given and unconditional.

This is the meaning of the fragrance of the rose.
This is what I removed from the garden when the rosebush died.
This is what I lost when Claudette moved out.

Chapter 4
Part I:
The Sign of Fidelity

> "Perhaps the soft breeze of midnight
> has become Gabriel, so that...the
> trees could become Mary."
> Kisa'i, (11th Century Persian poet)

The night Claudette left me, I sat up late and watched the slides of our trip to Europe, the trip we took in the summer of 1971 just after Claudette moved into my house. This was the trip on which we made a devout promise to each other which became our marriage vow. I had used many of the slides from that trip, the ones of paintings and frescoes and architectural details, to demonstrate my lectures.

I watched the slides again that night and grieved that the aspiration of our union could not be achieved now. Our aspiration was to sainthood. More accurately, our aspiration was to an embodiment of sainthood through love-making. Frankly, this aspiration to sainthood started as a joke, because, as we toured through the cathedrals and galleries of Europe, we started teasing each other about which representation of the saints and deities we thought we resembled most during love-making. We were recognizing each other's intimate expressions in the sublime ecstasies depicted on the faces of all the saints. We were experiencing these same ecstasies in the beds of Siena and Assisi, Cologne and Paris, and even in the small village of Douai in Alsace where we spent the night before travelling to the English Channel and crossing to Dover.

Ten years later, on the night Claudette moved out, I watched the slides of Europe over and over again. I spent the longest time on the slide of Our Lady of Perugia. That's where the process began, at *The National Gallery of Umbria* in Perugia, when I saw the statue of Our Lady move.

I am holding that slide in my hand now. I took the picture immediately after I saw the statue move, having wondered for years why the slide did not capture anything of that miraculous event. Whenever I look at it - whether I am holding it up to the light of the sun, as I am now, or whether I am showing it to a class - I expect to see Our Lady move again, to incline her head slightly to one side, as if pointing someone out to me.

That's how it happened in Perugia. I was looking at the painted wood-carving of the Madonna, and Claudette was somewhere else or in another room. I reached out toward the carving. I wanted to touch her hand. Then Our Lady inclined her head slightly to one side, and I looked in the direction she indicated and saw Claudette looking out the window, as if trying to see the blue of the Mediterranean Sea across the Umbrian Plain. I looked back at Our Lady, and she was still again. My hand was touching the blue of her robe . It was the same blue as the blue of the sky above the Mediterranean Sea. I stepped back and took a picture. I'm looking at that picture now. I am holding the slide up to the light of the sun, and there is no slight inclination of the head to one side. But for a moment in 1971, it moved. And I knew I was in love.

The next day, in Assisi, I proposed to Claudette. We have told the story many times to many people in many different situations. Mostly we told it to each other.

We were in the Basilica of Saint Francis, in Assisi, looking at the Giotto murals depicting the life of Saint Francis. In front of the mural depicting Saint Claire as she held a reclining Saint Francis at the moment of his death, (Mural 15), I went down on one knee and asked Claudette to marry me.

When Claudette tells it, I am the Angel Gabriel, and the two of us are exact re-creations of the figures in another fresco, *The Annunciation*, by Fra Angelico, (a print of which we had bought already at Saint Mark's in Florence). Claudette had both hands crossed over her heart, and I had my left knee bent, with my right hand over my heart. This is how Fra Angelico depicts the angel Gabriel, in marked contrast to the other artist-monk Fra Filippo Lippi who depicts the angel with the left hand over the heart.

I did some research on this, and according to J.S.M. Ward in *The Sign Language of the Mysteries*, one hand held over the heart is 'the sign of Fidelity'. Further, according to Ward, and in support of Claudette's observation, this sign can be made with either the left hand or the right hand. Although, when the hand is clenched, as if gripping the flesh above the heart, this is another sign altogether, 'the tearing out of the heart',which is usually associated with depictions of *The Resurrection* or *The Last Judgement*. When both hands are crossed over the heart, most properly with the left hand on top of the right (Claudette's posture exactly), this is 'the sign of Acceptance', the sign associated, almost exclusively, with Our Lady in scenes of *The Annunciation*.

Claudette said that at the exact moment when I went down on one knee and proposed to her, she had been contemplating the faces of Saint Claire and Saint Francis, wondering why such sublime love in a man and a woman towards God, was never given physical expression to one another in the body. There were tears in her eyes because the love of the two saints had not been allowed to live in the world as an intense physical passion between them.

We vowed that this passion would live in our marriage. What roots the impulse for God to Earth? What anchors the fluttering heart inside a body? My body remembers. It remembers, for instance, the passion I had with Claudette in Italy, and France, and England briefly. For an entire month we became saints who brought heaven's love to each other in bodies. We were the god and goddess representing the firmament: me the heavens and Claudette the Earth. Or, I was the nightingale and Claudette was the rose drawing me down into her Persian garden. We ached from our love, and the more we ached, the more we held close the thing that caused the ache. [1]

My body remembers. Passion is a body memory. Is there anything other than the body that can remember and hold to things like the body holds? Most days I don't think I remember anything at all anymore, but merely rearrange figures in a tableau, figures inside me like Mary and the posing angel, who know everything about each other because they have posed together in every scene ever painted, and simply move in and out of studied positions, (Nativities, Ascensions, or Assumptions-of-the-dead), moving with such ease and grace from one tableau to another, that they look like they're dancing. But when the dancing movement is frozen in a moment, the moment becomes a scene, and the scene becomes an attitude when the mind falls in love with it, and holds it close, and won't let it move away again.

Did the Angel Gabriel *cause* Mary to assume the sign of Acceptance, or was she in that posture already and always, because she was Mary, or had she been following a discipline, a daily practice, preparing for this moment? Did the Angel Gabriel assume his position because of the significance of his message, or did he kneel automatically in the presence of such a one as Mary? Isn't it true then, that the Annunciation is an attitude of the heart, an attitude of Fra Angelico's heart?

Claudette has blue eyes. They are the blue of the sky and the sea.

---

[1] "The pain was so great that I screamed aloud, but felt such infinite sweetness that I wished the pain to last forever." (Teresa of Avila, *Life*.)

Chapter 4
Part II:
The Sign of Sleep

> "*The Sign of Sleep* is made with the
> index finger of the left hand pressing
> on the right nostril. This indicates
> the semi-consciousness of normal
> waking life."
> *The Sign Language of the Mysteries*,
> J.S.M. Ward.

When we got home from Italy, Claudette and I had a fierce argument about which print of *The Annunciation* we should hang in our bedroom to commemorate my proposal to her in Assisi: Claudette wanted Fra Filippo Lippi's *Annunciation* and I wanted Fra Angelico's . I won the argument. Basically, Claudette's reasoning lacked any aesthetic consideration: she preferred the painting by Filippo Lippi, (who was a student of Fra Angelico and whose work is highly derivative - if not totally imitative - of Angelico), because she liked the story behind the painting! I was appalled. Claudette liked the fact that Filippo Lippi had fallen in love with his model for the Madonna and that they had run off together and had had a child in Venice. Personally, I have never liked Filippo Lippi as a painter. He is considered more sophisticated than Angelico because he understood the scale of the new large paintings of the Renaissance, (whereas Angelico's paintings still looked like enlargements of manuscript drawings), but I had always felt that he was an opportunist who took the sublime quality of Angelico's work and popularized it by putting more figures in the image area and adding more arches to the buildings and more folds to the gowns. This reasoning held little sway with Claudette. I only won the argument by reminding her that when she saw me go down on one knee in front of her in Assisi she had been instantly reminded of the Archangel Gabriel in Angelico's *Annunciation*. "Therefore," I said, "that is the print we must have in our bedroom."

Claudette had often told me how difficult it was to live with me. I certainly found it difficult to live with her, especially at the end when she became so explosive and unpredictable. But I found it even more difficult to live without her. I hardly slept.

Night after night I would lie awake staring at the Fra Angelico print of *The Annunciation* on the bedroom wall, or I would go to the studio at the back of the house and watch the slides of Europe over and over again, or I would stay in bed and thumb through my old manuscript *The History of the Rosary* from front to back, and then from back to front again.

Let me describe one moment of that winter, a moment which contains the nature of that entire year of Emptiness. It was a moment of stillness and night, when I felt utterly alone in the house, and the snow covered the garden in the backyard, and a glaze of ice covered the snow, and there wasn't a mark on anything anywhere, and the linden creaked suddenly and woke me from a still dream, and I went to stand at the window, and in that moment the moon was the moon, and suddenly, nothing miraculous happened.

I longed for a miracle that winter, but nothing happened to confirm my connection with heaven and with the saints. Back then, in 1981, I was unable to hold myself in my body for sustained periods. I had "a disruption occurring at the ankles", (see Introduction 1), and I felt more comfortable at a place slightly removed where I could observe myself and others, and make comments, commenting largely because I held a large perspective, observing the entire history of Western culture as if from the ridge-line at the top of my house while it occurred in the various sections of the garden in my back yard.

In the dream I had that winter night in 1981, the dream from which the creaking of the linden woke me, I saw the light of the moon falling into my walled garden, but in the dream the garden was totally different than it was in reality: the symmetrical plots were gone and there was a sunken garden in the middle surrounded by a circle of trees and at the centre of the sunken garden was a flat black stone. The light in my dream was coming from the moon, but it was really a supernatural light that had appeared in my dreams for many years. I had always allowed the light to lead me upward and I would get lost in it. But that night the light was reflecting from the ice and the snow in the sunken garden and from the blackness of the stone at the centre, so the more I fell into the light, the more I fell into the garden and into the stone. I fell into matter. I fell beneath the surface of the Earth. I fell down and down to the hot molten core at the centre of the Earth, to the heart of matter, to where nothing could be reduced to something less than itself anymore.

Nothing was alterable there, and everything was still, and everything hummed in the tension that kept things where they were and separate, and all that could change anymore was my relationship to it all. So I found myself moving deeper and deeper into the still and humming tension, which grew and grew and became as if more inalterable, until I heard a loud cracking sound near me or with in me, which woke me up, and which I assumed at once was the linden trying to sway in the stiff silence outside.

I went to stand at the window, and I could see the moon. The moonlight was on the garden, on the ice on the snow. The moon was the moon. It was just like the moon.

I would do this often, look into the light, in my still dreams or in my waking, as a way of discerning a means of escape. I was looking for escape from my body. This started when Claudette moved out, but really I had been looking for escape since I was an infant. Mostly I would look up into the light. I aspired to heaven. I wanted to escape to a transcendent place.

When Claudette moved out, my year of Emptiness began. And my travel to the edges of the universe became more intense, as if I was moving around the perimeter, as if looking inward from the margin that surrounds matter, trying to find the point of perfect perspective that would make sense of this life. But in all my travelling, and in all my looking, I never found myself in heaven, only at the curvature of space, the furthest point of matter, where my fingers would reach up and scrape the dome of the thing containing me.

Then I would look down from there, as if down, and see the Earth far below. The Earth was like a Lady with her hands crossed over her heart (her left hand on top of her right) and her arms would open instantly when she saw me, and she would hold them open to embrace me, and I would fall to her, as if falling and continuing to fall, until something made a cracking sound near me or inside me, and I was in a garden where no footprints marked the still and perfect cold, and I was standing motionless, the way the linden stands motionless, squirming inside myself like someone embraced too tightly. I was squirming out of the sleep state, squirming out of the arms of the Lady holding me too tightly.

Before that night, moonlight on snow had been like the point of brilliance in an angel's eye. On that night I was fooled by it: the light no longer led me to heaven, but downward into the heart of matter.

Many people before me have been fooled by heaven. They have felt betrayed, as if left just outside the gates of paradise, left naked on a large stone in a cold wind under grey skies, with only the stone to love them, and only the clouds to cover them, and only their own tears to warm them, while the angels looked down indifferently.

My experience was only slightly different. I experienced being left outside the gates of paradise in the cold, until I felt the pinpoint of its intensity piercing me at the heart, making me weep until I thirsted from weeping, and then my tears froze just as they reached my tongue.

That was how I fell through the shadow of the hole left by the rosebush, how I fell through the hole where my centre should have been.

When these dreams of falling ended, I wept. I wept because I knew I would never achieve Heaven now.

Never.

Then I wept because of what I saw at the threshold of Heaven, when I paused at the extremity of matter, just before I began falling into the arms of the Lady: Heaven was empty. Everyone had left, had fallen, (had begun falling centuries ago - on the day Fra Angelico finished painting *The Annunciation*), and they continue to fall until they can fall no further. They fall onto continents and onto peninsulas and islands, onto stony land without trees at the centre of islands, onto the rocky shores of those islands where frozen rivers meet frozen seas, and they pray there together and starve there together from generation to generation, and they fall into gardens, into the garden behind my house. They are angels awakening to discover they are Gabriel, but Gabriel carved from the wood of a linden, one knee bent, both wings missing, one hand placed gently over the heart, alone and awkward in a stranger's garden, on the coldest night of the year.

Gardening is an exercise that has greatly helped me in this condition. I used to hate gardening. The only work I ever did in the garden — after ten years of letting Claudette take care of everything — was dig the rosebush out of the ground. I didn't even know the names of any flowers or trees. Then, in the Spring following Claudette's move out of the house, I began to realize that gardening is a spiritual practice devised for angels who have landed awkwardly on the Earth. It helps bind them gently to a specific place, and tends to be beneficial for all of us who fear this enclosure of the Earth, and who resent being embraced too tightly by the Lady who drew us here from our home in paradise.

Chapter 4
Part III:
The Sign of Sorrow

> "When you come before the face of
> the Virgin Inviolate, be sure to utter
> an Ave as you pass."
> (Translation of the Inscription at the
> bottom of *The Annunciation*,
> Fra Angelico.)

My year of Emptiness ended when Spring came to the garden. Specifically, it ended when an event occurred that I call "the miracle of the rose". The miracle occurred in the exact same place that I had dug out the rosebush a year earlier.

This is what happened:

I was standing on the back porch in the late morning sunshine wondering who I could hire to take care of the garden. You'll remember that I didn't know anything about gardening at this point, except that this particular garden was filled with perennials and so wouldn't take much care, but I didn't even know the names of the annuals that Claudette planted "to cover the gaps when one perennial has faded and the next one hasn't quite started flowering" - ("impatients", of course). I looked around the yard and saw the tips of the blue flowers ("blue scilla") that had popped up overnight on the narrow strips of grass beside the central pathway, and saw the buds of the yellow shrubs against the stone wall of the garden near the house ("forsythia shrubs"), and wondered if everything was always out so early in the year.

Then I saw her. I saw the Lady standing at the bottom of the garden in the place where Tante Huguette's rosebush used to be. I started walking towards her, then stopped all at once when I reached the midpoint of the central path in the middle of the garden: the Lady looked exactly like "The Lady of Perugia" whose statue had moved miraculously ten years earlier.

I smelled the perfume of spirea or lilac. I saw that the Lady was wearing the same long cape that she had worn in Italy, but that it was now of deep blue, the deep blue of the sky on winter nights, and that she wore nothing underneath the cape so that I could see the outline of her breasts and the darkness of the hair between her legs where the perfume was coming from. She was beautiful. I heard a cracking sound, the cracking that comes from deep inside your heart on winter nights because an intense point of cold has split you at the chest and you cannot squirm away from the stillness penetrating you.

This was the Lady from the heart of matter who had been coming to me in my dreams all winter. Like moonlight on ice. Some people call her *The Lady who Pierces the Heart with Cold.* I call her *The Lady of the North.*

The Lady bowed her head toward me then knelt gently on one knee and took her right arm from beneath her deep blue cape and in her hand there was a rose which she placed gently over her heart. She took her left arm from beneath her cape and it was missing from the elbow. Her left arm was missing from the elbow, but she continued to move it as if making a gesture with the missing hand. She looked me directly in the eye and spoke briefly, then bent and kissed the Earth, and rolled onto her back so that her deep blue cape fell away from her body completely. She moved her body rhythmically and sensually as if someone was making love to her, and then she was gone.

The sun went behind a cloud and the shadows in the garden faded. Then the sun came out again and the patches of shade on the ground grew even more distinct than they had been before, and I saw that I was standing in the shadow of the trunk of the linden.

What did Fra Angelico do after he finished painting *The Annunciation*? I stood alone at the centre of the garden staring at the place where Tante Huguette's rosebush used to be. I wanted to understand the message that the Lady had just given me, but she had not made her gesture with the usual clarity that I had come to associate with all her representations in icons, frescoes, and oil paintings. "What is the gesture you were making with your missing arm?" I said to the empty space where the Lady had been standing.

Then I saw it. I saw my miracle. I walked quickly to the place where the Lady had been standing (three feet to the left of where I had dug out Tante Huguette's rosebush one year earlier), and there it was: a small shoot was coming out of the ground with something budding on it. The small shoot was like a twig, and that was my miracle. To be perfectly honest, I didn't recognize it as a miracle until three hours later when Claudette came walking into the yard, having decided, just that afternoon, to come back and visit her garden. She was dressed entirely in black. She bent down quickly and looked closely at the small budding twig, then stood up and told me that it was a rose shoot and that it must have come from Tante Huguette's rosebush.

Claudette didn't think this was a miracle. Rose plants send out underground suckers all the time she said, that's how they spread. In fact, she didn't want to discuss the new rose shoot at all. "Roses remind me of Tante Huguette," she said, "and Tante Huguette isn't with me anymore. I think something disturbing and terrible has happened to her." (See Chapter 7 for the details of this story.)

Claudette explained that her relationship with Tante Huguette was inseparably connected with her relationship with me, and that the two inter-relationships, once understood, explained why our marriage ended, and what was going to happen to us now. "Everything is intertwined." she said.

We drank wine on the back porch, then opened another bottle and drank that while talking in the kitchen, as the house grew dark around us. Claudette didn't leave until the next morning. In fact, I made love to Claudette that night. She had been planning to take the 11:00 commuter flight back to Montreal, but when we finished talking, and looked at the clock (and looked at each other), it was midnight. There was only one light on in the entire house, that little one above the clock on the top of the kitchen stove.

For my part, I was both shaken and delighted by my miracle. I didn't understand the nature of it really, having assumed that all miracles came from heaven, while, quite clearly, this one had arisen from out of the Earth.

I knew that the resurrection of the rosebush was connected with the visitation of the Lady, but I also knew that neither of these events, when taken on their own, could be considered miraculous. The same was true even when these two events were considered along with Claudette's unannounced arrival the very same day. I was convinced, however, that there was a miracle. Then, finally, at midnight in the kitchen, looking at the little light above the clock on the stove, I saw it: the three events, (the annunciation by the Lady, Claudette's visitation, and the resurrection of the original rosebush), were three inter-related signs pointing to the real miracle which hadn't happened quite yet: Claudette and I were getting together again. The arm missing from the Lady was a symbol of the wound our marriage had suffered. Then, as our marriage was renewed, the Lady would grow a new arm, and in the hand of this new arm she would hold the secret to everything. I even let myself believe - for a brief moment - that in order to make our reconciliation permanent, I would have to develop a new spiritual practice, the practice of a gardener.

I hated gardening, but I was desperate for Claudette to move back, and I was worn out by the grief and desolation I felt at the heart of matter where the pinpoint of cold pierced my heart repeatedly and cracked me open and filled me with a deeper and deeper cold. All I wanted was for everything to be alright again.

How could the Lady of the North (who pierced my heart all winter), be the same Lady as the beautiful and wounded Lady of the Rose? Was the Lady herself giving me the answer when she bent and kissed the ground before rolling onto her back in my walled garden?

Was she showing me that roses grow only when blessed with the intense and motionless cold that pushes everything to its outer limit, to its curvature, where it bends back into itself, and falls. As if falling and giving in to her.

Can you find the miracle here? Roses do not bud in April. Roses are not supposed to grow on the Gaspé either. The native wild rose grows there of course, but not the European hybrid strains, like the Fragrant Cloud, as planted by Tante Huguette in the summer of her death.

Can you identify the moment when the miracle happened? As I write this now in the sunlight in the grove at the back of the garden, surrounded by the climbing hydrangea and the hollyhocks and the blossoms of the rose-of-sharon, I would say that the miracle occurred just as the Lady kissed the ground. This was her way of telling me that if I want the energy of the saints, I must learn to want what the saints want, which is Her.

Who was the first saint who fell to Earth? Who was the first one who was ready to achieve heaven, but who paused in the final moment, in the pure pinpoint of cold at the threshold of matter, looked to Earth, then fell back in love. And when falling, fell to Her: heaven's sweet beloved.

Yes, it was the Archangel Gabriel in Fra Angelico's *The Annunciation*. Gabriel has knelt speechless for five hundred years in the face of the Lady who drew him here.

The Lady waits. That is the miracle. She waits for all us saints. She waits while we fall, waiting as if naked from the scented bath (her hair up, her body powdered and perfumed). And we fall (as if falling and continuing to fall), until something cracks near us or within us. And this cracking is our hearts splitting, it is the Earth opening because something new is growing. It began growing when the crust of the Earth split, and a crack appeared in somebody's sidewalk in the late afternoon shade at the side of a house under screened windows, while the house grew dark and two people talked, holding glasses full of wine, resting a head in a hand with the elbow on the table, extending an arm and bending it so the palm rests on a forehead, placing a hand over a heart then leaning forward across a table, both of them weeping because they are not very good at making the mantric signs anymore, as if one of them has an arm missing and the other one is still frozen in disbelief that he is here at all, in a kitchen where, on the other side of the room, above the stove, a little light shines.

3rd Purport:
The Sign of Acceptance

> "Fra Angelico's representation of the
> angel Gabriel is perhaps something
> less majestic than is usual with the
> painter." John Ruskin, describing the
> angel Gabriel in Fra Angelico's *The
> Annunciation*. Museo di San Marco,
> Florence.

Suffering has been a large part of my life, and I don't like to talk too much about it. It becomes the only thing people remember about me. That is why I decided to describe the events that led to the appearance of the Lady in my garden, but not to describe the quality of my suffering during that period, (beginning with the death of the rosebush, followed by Claudette's move to Montreal, then concluding with her surprise visit the next Spring).

When I was nine years old I had an operation on my heart. It left a scar on my chest and on the upper portion of my abdomen. Because of the quantity of hair on my chest now, the only part of the scar visible anymore is that upon my upper abdomen. I should have died before I was ten.

I wanted to die. I had never taken root very well in my body. The operation I had when I was nine was not a success, and they wanted to operate again. That was when I met the Lady, the Lady I have called Our Lady of the North, who came to me in the deep dreams I had as I was deciding, in myself, whether or not I should go through a second operation or just leave this world entirely.

The Lady brought me to that place I described in Chapter 4, Part II, as "the curvature of space", and "the threshold of heaven". Then she turned me around and showed me the Earth which she said she loved and which she said was Her. Then she took me down to the Earth and showed me an image of a woman seated in a sunken garden surrounded by flowering roses. Years later I recognized this woman in the statue of Our Lady of Perugia, and then again as the wounded Lady of the Rose who came naked into my walled garden. But in the dream when I was ten, the Lady of the Rose was seated with her legs crossed and with both hands cradled at the abdomen. She was repeating a name or phrase over and over silently with her lips. Her eyes were focused on her hands. A clear black fluid was collecting in her hands, and I could see that this fluid contained the mystery of my suffering. It was the liquid essence of physical life. And then the Lady raised me to her breast and I began to suck. I sucked and I sucked at the Lady's breast for the rest of the night, while she stroked my head as if I was a baby.

When I woke up from that dream, I felt that the Lady was inside me, seated heavily in my abdomen, draining away the fluid that had collected around my heart. That's when I knew I would live. To be perfectly honest, I made my decision to stay here not for myself, but for Her. She showed more concern and love for me than I had ever felt for myself. I decided that if she loved me so much, I would love her. Then, possibly, I could find what it was in myself that she could love so much.

I didn't need a second operation. The hole between the two ventricles of my heart healed on its own. When you know something like this about a person, it can be the only thing you remember about them. That's why I don't like to tell this story often. This may be the only time I refer to it.

But, imagine that this isn't a true story. Imagine that it never happened and that I have made it up in order to provide a precedent for the Lady's appearance in my life at the time of my marriage break-up. Imagine that this story is an analogy for the quality of my suffering at the time my marriage ended and I met the Lady of the North who had nothing kind to teach me.

What sort of person would make up a story like this?

What is the nature of suffering that it would make me create a Lady to carry its image for me?

The Earth is like a broken heart. Whenever something new grows from it, it breaks a little more. It cracks to allow space for the new life. I learned that if I didn't allow my own heart to break, nothing new would happen. And unless I loved the Lady of the Rose I would never understand that my heart was not my own, that my heart was just an empty garden, walled and private, into which I must bring Augustine Baker and the Lady of the Rose. You see, I learned that my heart was a walled garden that I was preparing for Augustine Baker and the Lady of the Rose, like a marriage chamber scented with the blossoms of lilies and spierea, with petals of lilacs and roses, that drift downward on a breeze.

Let me clarify this last image by telling you something that I couldn't tell you before. Let me tell you what the Lady said to me when she knelt gently on one knee, and placed a hand over her heart, and removed her wounded arm from beneath her deep blue cape, and kissed the ground at the back of the garden beside the new shoot of Tante Huguette's rosebush.

As she knelt on one knee and looked right at me, she said: "You must be the gardener. I have been looking for you for a long time. Help me prepare the garden for Him, for the One who will come, the King."

I couldn't have mentioned this message any earlier in the text. It wouldn't have been important unless I explained that the Lady was holding my life for me until I was ready to hold it for myself.

Nevertheless, I did not want to be the gardener.

I knew that I had been falling rapidly to Earth all winter, falling heavily into my body. But I didn't understand yet that I was also falling completely in love with the Lady, which meant that as I fell in love with her she was leaving my life in her old form, that is, I was no longer seated on her lap which had been a throne for me: I was no longer her little king.

Two things were very clear in the Lady's message: first, I had to find the real King and learn to serve Him, because only the real King could teach me how to love the Lady; and second, loving the Lady would be something like gardening.

Heaven was emptied of all us angels long ago, and we fell down to the Lady, we fell down in love. But then we turned bitter at the trap she became for us. And the more we tried to escape back to paradise, the tighter she held on - in desperation and pain - until, at last, we cut the tight embrace of her arms. She bears the wounds until this day.

My walled garden is the marriage bed I prepare for the King and Queen. But the King is always preceded by Gabriel. Gabriel is approaching one more time, announcing that an old lover from the stars is falling again.

Chapter 5
(for the Forty martyrs of
England & Wales 1535-1680)

"We are to speak nothing but truth in
the august presence of kings."
Gulistan, (Chptr 1, story 1); Sadi.

I need to tell you one more thing before I end the first half of the
novel. I need to tell you about my father, and about how my father is related to the Archangel Gabriel. You see, I have a picture of my father on the
wall of my bedroom facing the bed. There are two framed images on that
wall: there is the large print of Fra Angelico's *Annunciation*, and, directly
beside it, a small framed photograph of my father standing next to the King
of England. My father and the King are in the courtyard of Buckingham
Palace in London, and my father is receiving his medal from the King.
Only after Claudette moved out of the house, and only after I had spent so
many sleepless nights staring at the wall across from my bed, did I recognize a direct relationship between the image of my father in one picture and
the image of the Archangel Gabriel in the one next to it.

The house I live in, the house with the walled garden in the
back, was something I inherited from my mother. For a long time I was
unable to decide if the house was something she gave to me, or was
something my father gave to her to give to me.

My father died in a spectacular airplane wreck in Manitoba
when I was five. My mother was a dancer. She had met my father in the
early Autumn of 1940, in London, during the Battle of Britain. She was
dancing in the West End, and my father was an officer with the RCAF.
He met my mother when he came to London to get his medal and meet
the King. I was born a year later.

My father bought our house when he came back to Canada. I got
the house when my mother died. Things have always come easily to me.

It was when I lay awake staring at the picture of my father next
to the picture of The Annunciation, on the longest night of my winter of
darkness, the night when I went to the threshold of heaven and found it
empty, that I saw the significance of Augustine Baker's first appearance
to me in the walled garden. As you will remember from Introduction 2,
Baker arrived in the garden in the moment of pause when the knot of
rosebush root reached the furthest extension of my arms, and he entered
just after a thorn from the Lady of the Laurel Hedge stuck in my foot as

the Lady danced upward into the garden. Augustine Baker came and stood behind me, and I took a handkerchief from my pocket to wipe my forehead, and my father's coin fell into the hole in the ground where the rosebush used to be. Augustine Baker was magnificent. He stood like the figure of Lazarus in *The Raising of Lazarus by* di Paolo, his arms held in the attitude of the figure of Christ in the altarpiece *Resurrection* panel by Gunewald, at Isenheim Cathedral. The Lady, on the other hand, was like the shade from something think and tangled, or the shadow of a storm.

It was when I lay awake on the longest night of winter, with my manuscript on the History of the Rosary on my lap, staring at the picture of my father on the far wall, that I realised, all at once, that I was the Archangel Gabriel. I realised, specifically, that I was the Archangel Gabriel whom Fra Angelico brought to Earth for his painting of *The Annunciation* at the monastery of San Marco in Florence. And I realised that Augustine Baker was my King, and that Augustine Baker wanted me to make my Annunciation to the Lady of the Laurel Hedge. He had met her in the garden of Philip Fursden three hundred years before and had dismissed her as the work of the devil and had ascended toward Heaven. Now he was back to see her again. He wanted a reconciliation. I was to be Gabriel.

I kept staring at the photograph of my father on the wall, and then kept staring at the painting of *The Annunciation* next to it. Then I got out of bed and walked up to them and put one hand on the image of the Archangel Gabriel and the other hand on the image of my father. I could see how much I was like him, and I could see the link between us. The link was so obvious, but I had never seen it before: we were both in service to a King. My father's King was George VI of England, and my King was Augustine Baker. Baker wanted me to bear a message to the Lady of the Laurel Hedge. He had said to me: "Find out if she still likes dancing." Then he had added quietly: "I am terrible at dancing. Why is dancing more difficult than flying?"

Augustine Baker had not danced for three hundred years. He had stopped dancing in the garden of Philip Fursden when he rejected the Lady of the Laurel Hedge. Since then the fluid motion of his dance had become frozen into an attitude. Ascension was the attitude Augustine Baker had about dancing.

We are to speak nothing but truth in the kingly presence of the august.

I realised that by arranging the marriage between Augustine Baker and the Lady of the Laurel Hadge, I was completing the work started by Gabriel in the fifteenth century. But I was to be Gabriel in a scene of Annunciation utterly different from the one painted by Fra Angelico. This new Gabriel was frightened, the King himself was crippled at the ankles, and the Lady who was to receive the message was missing the left arm at the elbow.

In the photograph of my father standing with the King they are facing each other and they are talking. "What shall you do when you leave here today?" the King had asked. "Go dancing," my father had said. And that's how my father met my mother.

Book II

Chapter 6

> "...iconography constructs an image as
> one builds up a sentence or a discourse,
> by using elements of different origin and
> combining them according to practices
> comparable to the rules of grammar."
> *Christian Iconography, (A Study of its*
> *Origins)*, Andre Grabar.

The King has entered the novel. This could not have happened at just any point in the narrative. The text had to be ready for him. The new central metaphor had to be in place.

As you know, the novel began with the removal of its central metaphor, and with the expressed formal intention of discovering a new metaphor that would bind the elements together in a centripetal configuration around it, giving new meaning to the events that were occurring in my life at that time. I knew that the new metaphor would have to fit exactly into the hole I had dug when I removed the original rosebush, so I expected the new metaphor to be something similar to the rose (perhaps a strain of hybrid rose other than the original Fragrant Cloud, or the native wild rose itself), but I didn't expect the original rosebush to send up a new shoot into my walled garden the following Spring. Naturally I took this event as a sign that the resurrected rosebush was the novel's new central metaphor. I was mistaken, of course. I was mistaken about a great many things at that time. You see, the new central metaphor was not a rose at all, but was the shadow cast by the rose. Specifically, the new central metaphor of the novel was the hole in the ground that I had dug to remove Tante Huguette's rosebush from the garden in Introduction 1. The new metaphor was created through the very act of removing the old one. I should have expected that.

In fairness to myself, however, I must point out that the hole in the ground did not become the novel's new central metaphor right away. This did not happen until later in the novel, in Chapter 4 Part II: The Sign of Sleep. It happened in the sentence: *"Then I wept because of what I saw at the threshold of Heaven, when I paused at the extremity of matter, just before I began falling into the arms of the Lady: Heaven was empty."*

In this sentence the emptiness of the original hole in the ground in my walled garden entered Heaven, and Heaven too became empty. It was in that sentence that the hole in the ground began functioning as a metaphor, because, for the first time, it joined two unlike things together, the way metaphors have always joined unlike things together, in this case Heaven and Earth.

When you were reading Chapter 4, Part II, did you realize that you had arrived at the centre of the pattern that the novel was forming, as if it was the pattern of a Persian carpet from Iran woven in the style of the Tabriz area? And did you realize that by reading that sentence, the one quoted above, that you too had fallen into the emptiness?

It was in that sentence that the hole in the ground in my walled garden stopped being a point on the Earth and became an axis that went all the way from Heaven right down to the Earth. In fact, it passed through the Earth, and passed through the hot molten core at the centre of the Earth, and passed through the centre of my life. This is the axis that holds the world in place. The axis is hollow. It is a tube. It runs through the centre of the novel and holds the disparate elements together in a centripetal configuration around it.

The novel now has a new central metaphor and everything you are reading is spinning around it. The axis creates a link between Heaven and the depth of the Earth. It is down this corridor that Augustine Baker has fallen from Heaven. It is up this corridor that the Lady of the Laurel hedge has danced into my garden. The place of meeting of Augustine Baker and the Lady of the Laurel Hedge is an empty hole at the centre of my life. This "empty hole at the centre of my life" is, of course, the hole I dug to remove the rosebush. This empty hole is a metaphor. It is a metaphor for my empty heart. The phrase "empty heart", on the other hand, is not a metaphor. It is real. It is the actual meeting place of Heaven and Earth, the home that the King requires before he can enter the world from Heaven. "*Open* heart", however, *is* a metaphor. And "surgery" is a metaphor. Therefore the "open heart surgery" of my childhood, which I admitted to having invented in the *3rd Purport*, is also a metaphor, and it is directly connected to the novel's central metaphor: it created the hole in me that allowed the new central metaphor to pierce me and pass right through me. This is very important. It is the main point of this chapter: the same axis that passes through the centre of the novel passes through the hole in my heart.

In order to fully understand how these two images overlap you should imagine that I am lying face up in the garden where the rosebush used to be, and imagine that the axis that goes between Heaven and the depth of the Earth is plunging through my heart and pinning me down so that my empty heart and the hole in the ground are one. Therefore, when Augustine Baker and the Lady of the Laurel Hedge moved up and down the tunnel, my heart was their meeting place. Therefore, my heart is a walled garden half way between Heaven and the darkness at the depth of the Earth.

Chapter 7

> "The problem of giving work titles is a
> complicated and a personal problem...but
> I realized that the title could act as a
> metaphor to identify the emotional con
> tent or the emotional complex that I was
> in when I was doing the painting."
> Barnett Newman, (*Painters Painting*,
> Emile De Antonio).

There is a great deal I haven't told you yet, and which I need to tell you now, about what happened to Claudette after she moved out of my house on the eve of our tenth anniversary. As you will remember from Chapter 2, Claudette left me when the Lady in Black entered her life. What you don't know is that the Lady in Black told Claudette to leave. She told her to go back to Quebec, to visit the Gaspé, and then to go to Montreal and have her exhibition of new paintings there. When Claudette went back to Quebec she went through a major crisis, a crisis equivalent to my crisis at the threshold of Heaven where I saw that the saints had fallen and that Heaven was empty. Claudette's crisis occurred in Montreal. It occurred in three parts and the most significant part occurred in the old quarter of the city right on the banks of the St Lawrence River. It occurred when Claudette saw the face of the Lady in Black for the first time and saw that the Lady in Black was not Tante Huguette. It occurred on the night the Lady in Black tried to kill her.

Claudette left me because the Lady in Black told her to leave, and she had her exhibition of new paintings in Montreal because the Lady in Black told her to have it there. The exhibition was a great success - just like the Lady said it would be - and everything seemed to be going well for Claudette until that night down by the river. Claudette told me the whole story when we sat in the kitchen until midnight drinking two bottles of wine.

This is what she said:

"The whole transformation of my life started when I was still living with you and the Lady in Black entered my dreams. Right away she started teaching me about Sorrow. The Lady knows Sorrow. I mean, she *really* knows Sorrow. She says that sorrow belongs to women and that every woman must be close to it. Men know grief but only women know Sorrow.

"First the Lady in Black led me to the Gaspé, to the old family home in Rimouski. I still thought she was Tante Huguette at that point. I thought she was reminding me of the natural legacy of Sorrow that belongs to me as a daughter of Quebec. Then she led me to Montreal, to my new studio where I completed the work for my exhibition. I called the exhibition "The Seven Sorrows" in honour of my mother and her six sisters. You see, being back on the Gaspé put me in touch with the great sorrow of all women, and in particular with the sorrow of the women of Quebec, my ancestral mothers who brought sorrow with them from France and then found even more of it waiting for them here. We are haunted by sorrow and the land is haunted by it. Sorrow is a curse on the daughters of Quebec."

The Lady in Black was a voice inside Claudette. The Lady's voice contained the sorrow of all The Mothers. The Lady kept repeating a phrase or name over and over in Claudette's mind, and the voice grew louder and louder until finally, when Claudette's paintings were finished and she had put all the sorrow she had learned into the canvases, the voice became very very loud. Then Claudette's first crisis occurred. It occurred on the night her exhibition opened.

Her paintings were utterly different from anything she had done before. They were darker and more simple and direct. One critic compared Claudette's paintings to Barnett Newman's minimalist black-on-white *Stations of the Cross* series (first exhibited at the Guggenheim Gallery in 1960), and described Claudette's paintings as "meditations on the pure darkness of distilled shadow" . In fact, it was this same critic who brought Claudette to her first crisis. When he was interviewing her at the Opening of the exhibition he said that her paintings had the same "feeling tone" as his own meditations. He said that he was involved in a meditation circle that did a form of mantra meditation, or "imageless prayer" that involved repeating silently, over and over in the mind, the same phrase.

When he said this, Claudette's first crisis occurred. She said instantly and in a very loud voice: "Yes! Yes! We will be there! Yes! We will come!" They had both laughed at the intensity of her reply, and then they made arrangements to meet at the Meditation Centre on Pine Avenue at noon the next day. The crisis for Claudette was hearing the Lady in Black speak out loud through her for the first time.

The second part of the crisis occurred later that night. Claudette didn't sleep at all. The voice inside her wouldn't let her sleep. "My body was like a chapel filled with the voices of The Mothers saying a litany to the saints at a mass for the dead." She finally got out of bed and went outside one hour before dawn.

She wandered the streets of the old city half asleep and in a trance. She was following the Lady in Black. Then, just as the sun was beginning to lighten the sky, she found herself standing beside the river.

This is how Claudette tells it: "I followed the Lady down to the river where she stood at the edge of the water with her back to me. She had not been appearing to me visually, as a separate person, since I moved out of your house. I had come to know her only as a voice inside me. That morning was the first time I saw her face. It was a very dramatic scene. The Lady stood at the edge of the river and suddenly tilted her head back and began striking her forehead repeatedly with the open palm of her right hand. She was moaning in a desperate voice and she kept striking her forehead with her hand. Her gesture and her voice were filled with such sorrow that I wanted to hit her. I couldn't stand the sound of her voice any more, but she kept moaning and striking herself, and then she started to turn around and look at me. I expected to see the face of Tante Huguette, the face I had seen all my life when I prayed to her, a face like the face of my aunts or my mother. I thought the face might be older, perhaps much older, but instead it was young and beautiful, but beautiful in a different way from my mother's, and I didn't know this woman at all."

This was the second part of Claudette's crisis. She shouted at the Lady, "Who are you!?", and as she shouted she found that the Lady was gone and that she herself, Claudette, was standing at the edge of the river looking into the water.

"At that moment I felt a hand on my back and I knew that the Lady was going to push me into the river. I thought, 'I'm all alone with this stranger and I think she wants to kill me.' My feet were right on the edge of the cement retaining-wall. If she pushed , there was nothing left but falling.

"Then the hand on my back moved to my shoulder and pulled me back from the edge. I fell to the ground and I looked around and I was all alone. I noticed for the first time that I was directly behind the church of Notre Dame de Bon Secours, the church where Tante Huguette had been a nun. I looked up and saw the statue of the angel on top of the church. The angel was looking out over the St Lawrence and down the St Lawrence toward the sea . I thought, "You saved me! You are an angel sent by Tante Huguette from heaven to save me from the Lady in Black."

Claudette finished the story and shook her head back and forth. I noticed again that she was dressed entirely in black. Claudette looked at me, then put her elbows on the kitchen table and rested her head in the palms of her hands so that her fingers covered her eyes.

This was the point in the evening when I opened the second bottle of wine. It was the last of my 1970 Bordeaux. This particular vineyard produces a wine with a familiar robust quality which is, of course, the hallmark of all wines from over-ripe grapes. It has a nose, and a palate that is unconfused by subtleties.

I filled our wine glasses and said: "Let's drink to Tante Huguette who died last year and descended into hell, then rose again from the dead into my garden today."

We drank to that. I said: "You realize that there is a meaning to all this, and that the meaning is: you have to move back with me."

"That's the wrong meaning." Claudette. said.

"Tante Huguette is back", I said, "You saw the new rose shoot yourself, and that means that you must come back. Think about it: the Wounded Lady appeared to me on the exact spot of Tante Huguette's new rose shoot. And I was having my vision of her at the exact moment that you were getting on the plane to come here. The wounded Lady represents the wounds our marriage has suffered, and the new rose shoot represents a second chance we have. That's why you came back. Surely you can see that!"

"I'm not moving back." she said.

"Then take Huguette with you," I said. "If you want to ignore the meaning of everything that has happened today, take the new rose shoot back to Montreal where the original rosebush came from. In fact, put it back in the same garden at the Mother House on Rue St Jean Baptiste, in the exact same spot where Huguette dug it up to bring it to the Gaspé."

"Tante Huguette belongs here," she said.

"Yes," I said, "and so do you!"

"You don't understand the meaning of this at all." she said. "You think that Huguette's resurrection is a sign that you and I are getting together again. Well, that's not the meaning. Tante Huguette wants *you*! I learned that today when I saw the new rose shoot in your garden. Tante Huguette is bringing another message from heaven, but her message is for you this time, not me."

This was the best argument Claudette and I ever had. We had traded places: I was raising my voice and Claudette was struggling with meaning. The only other time I had gotten this angry with Claudette was during our marriage when she insisted that Fra Filippo Lippi was a greater artist than Fra Angelico. My argument had been sound on this point, but in fact, I was irrational about Filippo Lippi. Essentially my reason for considering him a lesser painter than Fra Angelico was the same reason as Claudette's for considering him a greater one: he took the woman who was his model for Mary in his painting of *The Annunciation* as his lover. I felt that this was a betrayal of the spiritual and creative purity that had entered the Renaissance with Fra Angelico. Besides, Filippo Lippi was arrogant and vain, and he had an almost childish need to get his own way - with the Church, or with his patrons, or with his model for Mary. Frankly, I hated to see this man compared to the high-minded and spiritual Fra Angelico. Of course I didn't tell Claudette that I now believed myself to be Fra Angelico's Archangel Gabriel. I thought she would interpret this simply as a clever new strategy on my part for achieving a place of unquestionable authority on Italian Art of the Renaissance.

Claudette leaned back in her chair and rubbed the open palm of her hand back and forth across her forehead. I reached across the table and took Claudette's glass and poured more wine.

There is something else I didn't tell Claudette. I didn't tell her about the emptiness that I had experienced after she moved out of my house. I was afraid she would feel sorry for me. During the worst periods of my emptiness I had pictured her happy in her new life, achieving critical attention already, (and from art reviewers other than me), attention that would lead to success with a more general audience. I had pictured her in a spacious studio/apartment overlooking old Montreal, discussing her future with art dealers from Paris and Cologne or New York. Instead, our separation had taken her to the edge of the world where she stood poised by a river and "all that was left was falling".

Claudette said: "After I went to the Meditation Centre on Pine Avenue I learned that Tante Huguette didn't save me from the Lady in Black by the river. Until today, until I saw the new rose shoot in your backyard, I thought I had lost Tante Huguette forever. But now I believe that something radical has happened, and it's all very clear to me: Tante Huguette has fallen from heaven - don't look so surprised - she has fallen from heaven, and she is bringing you an extremely important message of the greatest urgency. I mean look where she's landed: right in your walled garden."

"But if the Lady in Black isn't Tante Huguette", I said, "then who is she?"

"Now it's my turn to be surprised." she said. "The Lady in Black told me to come here today and that you would be able to tell me anything I wanted to know about her."

I made love to Claudette that night, and the saints were not with us anymore. I think that is all I can say for now about the story Claudette told me that night. I will tell you about the third part of her crisis in

Chapter 9. It explains everything that happened to Claudette from the moment she asked me to dig Tante Huguette's rosebush out of the garden.

I will say, however, that although I couldn't identify the Lady in Black yet, I did recognize the gesture that the Lady was making when she stood at the edge of the river in Montreal and tilted her head back and struck her forehead repeatedly with the palm of her open hand. This action is called the *Sign of Sorrow*. Sorrow can be traced as far back as ancient Egypt. It is the mantric sign associated almost exclusively with the goddess Isis in perpetual mourning for her consort Osiris whom she rescued from imprisonment in the Underworld after a lifetime of searching. [f]

For the remainder of the night Claudette and I were alone. There were just the two of us in the bedroom, but outside I could hear things moving uneasily in the garden. They moved sluggishly from under the shrubbery and climbed the trees and hung heavily from the limbs and swung back and forth outside the bedroom window, breaking off dead branches and throwing shadows against the window blinds. They were there in the wind, and in the storm, and in the dark of the night.

---

[f] See The Funeral Procession of Ani, from the Papyri of Ani *The Egyptian Book of the Dead*, Wallis Budge, Citadel Press, New Jersey.

4th Purport:
The crown of the King

> "King! let my words with thee
> find grace." Sadi, *Gulistan.*

I said earlier that I would likely never mention my heart operation again, the operation I had when I was nine years old, ("This may be the only time I refer to it." - 3rd Purport), but I need to say more about it already.

When the doctor came into my hospital room and told me and my mother that he wanted to do a second operation, he illustrated the situation by taking a coin from his pocket and holding it between the thumb and forefinger of one hand and pointing to it with the forefinger of his other hand and saying: "The hole between the ventricles of your heart is now just larger than the size of this quarter". He concluded that a hole that size was too large to close on its own. Then he left the room without giving me the quarter. I was nine years old and I liked quarters.

Then, as I've mentioned before, the Lady I now call *the Lady of the Rose* came to me in my dreams and began her healing activity around my heart. In the mornings after these dreams I would see a coin inside my chest, a coin exactly the size of a quarter. The coin would be very distinct at first and then it would fade away as I gradually woke up. I began the practice of holding the coin in my imagination as long as possible. I wanted to watch as it got smaller and smaller, as a way of watching the hole in my heart getting smaller and smaller. This did not happen. In fact, after a week the coin grew slightly larger and began to shimmer with a distinct brilliance. The brilliance was either coming from the coin itself or was reflected from something like the sun.

I stopped thinking about the coin immediately. I thought I was encouraging the hole in my heart instead of getting rid of it. Then my mother gave me something that changed my mind about this entirely. She gave me a coin just larger than the size of a quarter. It was a coin from England called a half-crown, and it was the exact same coin as the one I had been seeing inside my heart .

I had never felt close to my mother, probably because I was separated from her so much in my early life, but she helped me that day. She said:

"I thought you might like to have this. It was your father's good luck charm. He carried it in his tunic whenever he went up in one of his aeroplanes. It's about all they found of him after the crash. I've been afraid to give it to you really, because I thought that all the luck had run out of it. But still, it's something of your father's and that's what counts. He really believed it saved his life you know."

She looked at the coin, turned it over in her fingers, then put it into my hand. "If it got your father through the war, maybe it can get you through this."

You can understand why I needed to mention this incident. It shows the significance of my decision to leave this coin in the hole in the ground after I had removed the rosebush root. And it shows that the energy of the Lady and the energy of the Father are connected. But it doesn't answer other questions I have, for instance: was my father related to the Lady only through me, through his coincidence with her in my heart, or did they know each other before I was born; did the Lady help my father get through the war, or did She meet him only in the brief and sudden moment when my father's body was about to hit the Earth; and if the Lady did help my father get through the war, why did she let him crash five years later on the Canadian prairies? Does this mean that I must crash too? Does everyone she help crash eventually? Do they fall to Earth and burn until they are reduced to the essence of themselves, reduced to an amalgam of their precious elements which become heated to liquid then cooled and stamped with the image of the king.

Kings have always been made this way, through the fiery transformation of the elements existing in them. But the King cannot exist in the heart until an opening has been made there, a place created for him to occupy in the heart, and it is only the Lady who can create that opening, the emptiness at the centre of things. I have been told that when my father crashed into the prairies he made quite a hole in the earth. I believe now that it was my father's body I expected to find when I dug the hole in the ground in my back garden and removed the rosebush root from the earth in Introduction 1. And I believe that when I left the coin in the ground just as Augustine Baker arrived in the garden, I was completing the ritual that I had begun when I brought down the axe and cut the last of the rosebush roots, and that the ritual was one of transformation: I was transforming the longing that I had always had for my father, who I had hardly known, into a longing for my king.

Who is my king? Who is Augustine Baker? Who is this king I serve, this king I released from imprisonment in the Earth when I raised the rosebush root so carefully from that hole and held it in my hands and let go of my father and opened my heart to the king?

Chapter 8
A Speaking of God in the Soul

> "I must take heed that I, becoming a
> commentator upon an obscure work,
> become not more obscure in my
> exposition than the text itself which I
> would expound."
> Augustine Bakcr, (from the Introduction
> to *The Cloud of Unknowing*).

Augustine Baker had three "conversions" to the mystical way. These three conversions were the three brief moments in his life when he experienced the intense and shattering inner transformation called the "Union with God in the soul". Baker experienced each of these mystical transformations in a garden. His first conversion occurred in Italy when he was in the novitiate of the Benedictine Order, and I have often imagined that this first mystical experience took place while he was strolling aimlessly through the oldest botanic garden in Europe, the Orto Botanico at Padua, or while he was resting in the coolness of a courtyard garden in a ducal palace, or admiring the view from the top of the terraced garden of a Renaissance villa, perhaps one of the Medici villas like Castello or Petraia near Florence. Baker himself wrote very little about his first conversion and he never mentioned it to me personally whenever he came into my study on Sunday afternoons and sat in the wing-back chair, the one next to the fireplace, while we talked and looked out the French windows into the garden as the snow fell gently through the branches of the linden. He was never physically present of course, but he was present in spirit, and we communicated in a mental or prayerful way. That is how he would come to me in the night also, sitting in the chair beside my bed looking troubled, waiting to speak to me in the total quiet of the night when I would wake suddenly with a grunt or a moan from another dream of falling. I have always had to invent the details of Baker's first conversion in Italy, but I have known all about the other two conversions because Baker talked of them constantly. You see, his second and third conversions marked the beginning and the end of the most difficult period in his spiritual life, his "great desolation". Both his second and his third conversions took place in English country gardens.

Bakcr's "great desolation" was a twelve year period in which he was abandoned utterly by God. For these twelve years his heart ached with the torment of knowing that God had visited him in the deep intimacy of his heart, and then had left, had turned away and abandoned him utterly. For twelve years Baker was plagued by recurring periods of aridity and tormenting self-doubt. "There is no greater emptiness", he told me, "than the emptiness of a heart no longer filled with the intimacy of Him who you love so dearly." Baker's great desolation began immediately after his second conversion, when God filled his heart to bursting, then abandoned him totally. It happened when Baker sat in the garden of the Fortesque family near the village of Cookhill in the county of Worcestershire in the year 1608. Then, twelve years later, his great desolation finally ended when he experienced his third conversion in the garden of Philip Fursden near the village of Cadbury in the County of Devonshire in the year 1620. The Lady of the Laurel Hedge appeared naked to Baker in a vision. She stood at the bottom of the garden and she tried to tempt him from his route to God. Baker dismissed her as the work of the devil, and he was reunited with God, although in a mental or spiritual way this time, but was, by his own admission, "...not much subject to [further] aridities or desolations".[1]

I described Baker's third conversion in detail at the beginning of the novel in Introduction 2. When Baker dismissed the Lady of the Laurel Hedge as the work of the devil he cut himself free from the bonds of Earth, and remained in a transcended state for the rest of his life. He explained to me, however, that when he died he was not able to enter Heaven. He was drawn upward to God but he was also pulled simultaneously downward by the Lady of the Laurel Hedge. He felt suspended between the two worlds, and he hovered there for three hundred years.

When Augustine Baker sat beside my bed in the middle of the night he said: "After I died, at first I tried desperately to get the Lady to let go of me so I could be in heaven entirely, and then I started to realize, to my horror, that it was I who was holding on to her! Then I started looking for her everywhere. I went to the great gardens of the world, to the Alhambra at Granada in Spain, and the Hanging Gardens of Babylon, and even the formal, and overly fussy gardens of Versailles. I didn't find her anywhere. Then I began to notice that some gardens were held in a kind of stillness and others were not, so I started looking for the garden with the greatest stillness. I knew I would find the Lady of the Laurel Hedge there, and I knew that I would find you there - yes you - a gardener who was close to Her, a gardener who had been wounded in the foot by one of her thorns."

---

[1] *Life of Father Augustine Baker*, Cressy.

"But I am not the gardener," I said. "That day when I dug the rosebush out of the ground was the only time in ten years that ever worked in the garden."

"You are the gardener," he said. "When you toil in the garden you are like a bridge, a bridge between my light of heaven and the Lady's place of darkness."

Baker added that something in him was still drawn to the Lady of the Laurel Hedge - even after three hundred years - and that he didn't understand what the draw was, but that as a result of it his great desolation had never come to an end. Baker was very troubled by feeling so drawn to the Lady of the Laurel Hedge.

I told him that it was all very simple, that not only has heaven been closed, but God has fallen in love with the Lady of the Laurel Hedge and has begun falling down to Her. "Therefore," I said, "the closer you become to God, the closer you become to Her. That's why you're drawn to Her: you are feeling His draw, His attraction, His pull downward toward Her."

Baker said: "You have more faith in the darkness than I."

Whenever Baker said "darkness" he also meant "women" - more accurately, he meant his feeling of attraction to them. He felt that his great desolation was caused by a woman. "She kept me bound to this Earth when I wanted, so desperately, to be in Heaven."

During his life Baker wrote extensively about his "great desolation" and about its relationship to the profound mystical experience that caused it, and he did most of his writing when he was spiritual director of the English Benedictine nuns at Cambrai. He held this post for nine years. He wanted to understand what went wrong after his profound mystical union. He wanted to know what the relationship was between the love of God and love in general - which I took to mean the love for women. He wanted to place his mystical experience into the context of Christian prayer in general, and into the context of the monastic tradition of prayer in particular. He wanted to know why the monastic orders were so suspicious of the mystical experience of God's love, even though the mystical process was at the core of their community life going right back to the Desert Fathers in the first four centuries of Christianity. Essentially, Baker could not find anyone to teach him about love, about love itself, and could not find someone to tell him what went wrong after his deep and altering experience of his second conversion. He never found a teacher in the Benedictine Order to guide him in his spiritual life. Never.

The monastic orders found the mystical process impossible to supervise, and they considered it both anti-authoritarian and anarchic because it resulted in a deeply interior experience of God which required no outside authority to validate it, and because it presented truths which were, as often as not, far beyond the bounds of Church doctrine. As one Church father, a certain Cardinal Gasquet expressed it, ".. mysticism begins in mist and ends in schism."[2]

Because Baker never found a spiritual director to guide him in his inner life, he learned everything about the mystical process from books, so it wasn't until he came across the writings of an earlier master, (possibly one of the English mystics like Walter Hilton, or Richard Rolle, or the author of *The Cloud*), that he began to understand that his "great desolation" was an expected and predictable part of his process toward permanent illumination.

As the twentieth century spiritual scholar, Evelyn Underhill, points out "...the Object of the mystic's final quest and of his constant intuition is an object of adoration and supreme desire. ... For the mystic who has once known the Beatific Vision there can be no greater grief than ... the loss of this companionship, the extinction of this Light." [3]

This loss and extinction is the great desolation.

Now I am going to tell you of the tragedy that befell Augustine Baker during his second conversion: he fell in love. The tragedy was that Baker thought that by falling in love he had fallen from grace, and that he had ruined his spiritual life forever. The story takes place in the small town of Cookhill in the county of Worcestershire. It takes place in 1608 when Augustine Baker was sent to England as part of the missionary program of the Benedictine Order.

The English Mission of the Benedictines was designed to support and encourage the Catholic faith in England which was under heavy persecution from the protestant Parliament and the Church of England. Baker had been away from England for eight years training at the Benedictine centres at Paris and Rome. When he returned to England in 1608 it was still an act of treason against the crown to be a priest. It was punishable by death by beheading. Baker returned in secret, under another name, and in disguise as a lawyer.

The Benedictines had various systems of support for their priests on the English Mission. Baker was sent on the "Seigneurial" system, which meant that a priest was given financial support by a wealthy Catholic family in return for his personal chaplaincy of their household.

---

[2] Lunn, *The English Benedictines.*

[3] Underhill, *Mysticism.*

Baker was sent to the Fortesque family near the quiet village of Cookhill in Worcestershire. Among his duties was the task of guiding the prayer-life of Lord Fortesque's niece, the gifted and beautiful Elizabeth Fortesque, who was preparing to join the community of Benedictine nuns-in-exile in Cambrai, France.

As soon as Baker arrived at the Fortesque estate he launched on a disciplined program of contemplation. Baker believed that all monks on the English Mission should follow the practice of contemplation, that they should become "...perfect ambidexters, that is to say, suited as well for action as for contemplation."[4] He believed that a monk's spiritual life must be informed by this inner knowing. This was the practice he taught to Elizabeth.

After more than a year of this disciplined inner prayer Augustine Baker experienced his intense "illumination" which he called his second conversion: "God's work was most secret and profound, in the inmost centre of the spirit. [The] speaking of God...was an intellectual speaking such as angels may be supposed to practice to one another."[5] Baker thought he would never lose this intimacy with God. He thought the love would flow into his heart forever. His relationship with Elizabeth reached its flowering at this time. He remained pure with her, but he became as emotionally intimate as a lover.

The friendship with the young and beautiful Elizabeth had grown very close during the year of Baker's disciplined contemplation practice. Baker fell in love with Elizabeth when he achieved his illumination because in his open state he saw that all love was the love of God, and he saw that the feeling in his heart for Elizabeth was that same love. Elizabeth had greatly admired Baker before this, and they often walked aimlessly for hours in the garden talking about their shared love of God, but now she was enraptured with Baker, captivated by the love of God that filled his heart. How she loved him for loving God so much! Then suddenly, without warning, God's love stopped pouring into Baker's heart, and no matter what he tried he could not get it to flow again. Baker had begun his fall from grace. He stopped walking with Elizabeth in the garden, and in fact, he stopped talking to her altogether. He grew vague and careless, and finally Elizabeth heard from a servant that he had been arrested on suspicion of being a priest, that he had been arrested in one of the Public Houses he had been frequenting later - specifical-

---

[4] *The Treatise on the English Mission Benedictine*, Fr. Augustine Baker.

[5] *Life of Father Augustine Baker*, Cressy.

ly, in a house where he had been seen often in the company of women.

One of Baker's biographers, Herbert Sweeney, describes his fall from grace this way: "He found no comfort in God, and so sought it in creatures."[6]

Augustine Baker was thrown into prison. Elizabeth immediately took steps to effect his release. She thought only of how he had stood with her in the garden, in the fading light of the day, and had told her what God's love felt like in his heart, and said that when he looked in her eyes he felt the love grow stronger. The love of God is love itself. Love is all there is. Then they both felt the truth of this in a moment of pure clarity and understanding: they were bringing God's love into the world by loving each other. Elizabeth vowed never to betray that love. Baker vowed that he would take her away with him, and that they would go to Paris together or at least to London, where they could pursue their devotion to embodying God's love through a relationship with each other.

Augustine Baker almost died in prison. He almost became a martyr to the Catholic faith, but Elizabeth rescued him at the last moment and he was released from prison. Augustine Baker can be seen as one of the saints who went to the threshold of Heaven at the extremity of space, composed himself there in the formal stiffness, held himself in that moment of leaving, then came falling back to Earth in love. He can be seen as another Gabriel falling into the arms of the Lady who was calling him back to Earth. And Elizabeth can be seen as a metaphor for the Lady who stands with arms open wide waiting for him to fall into the sacred grove of her garden.

However, this would not be an accurate description of the situation. Baker wanted to die and enter Heaven. He wanted this desperately. Instead, he was turned away, and came falling back to his body and found it lying in prison, in Worcestershire. He had been conferring with the angels across the threshold that divides Heaven and Earth. He had been pleading with the angels to let him into Heaven. He had been pleading for weeks. He wanted to live in Heaven entirely, but the angels told him he must go back. He said he felt no desire for his body. They said he must be willing to hover near it at least, to be close enough to maintain identity, but that they would allow him to remain far enough away so that he didn't have to feel the pain of it. The real pain, he said, was being turned away from Heaven. "Go back," they said. And Baker came tumbling back to Earth, and as he tumbled into his body he saw the

---

[6] *Life of the Venerable Father Augustine Baker*, Sweeny.

keeper of the Jail standing over him, shaking him roughly, waking him as if from a deep, deep dream. The keeper was telling Baker that he could leave now, that a woman had come with papers setting him free. Baker was barely back in his body, but already he felt the pain of separation from heaven: "What must I do to leave this place!!" he said.

"You can leave immediately," the keeper said, "someone has secured your release." Baker shook his head and struck his chest repeatedly with both fists. "They will not undo these bonds." he said. "Tell me, how can I do it, how can I leave this place?!"

"Well sir, you can pick yourself up and walk straight through that door." the keeper said. "Now come along. She has vouched for you with papers."

In order to secure Baker's release Elizabeth had made a deal with the authorities. She agreed to sign the oath of allegiance as prescribed in the Anti-catholic Act of King James. The oath proclaimed allegiance to the Church of England, and it renounced support for papist missionaries from 'beyond the seas'. It was very offensive to Catholics in its wording. By signing the oath Elizabeth turned her back on the Catholic Church and renounced her own ambition to join the exiled Benedictine nuns in Cambrai, France. She had done this to be with Baker.

Baker didn't want to leave prison. Being held forceably in a cell without hope of release was an exact reflection of how he felt about having his soul held in his body against his will. "There is nothing in the world but cloud and darkness and not the least marks or footsteps of His presence".[7]

Elizabeth was afraid. She was afraid that by renouncing the Church she was renouncing God. She needed Baker to come back to her and reassure her that she was making the right decision, that they could really find the love of God together through their love of each other. She needed to hear again how their love for God which had been shared, or mutual, could now become embodied love which would be reciprocal, or held in common, expressible through each other's bodies which could still know grace.

She didn't understand the distinctions among reciprocal, mutual, and common.

She didn't understand that Baker was a different man, that he now experienced himself as crucified between Heaven and Earth, forbidden to live in the other world, and unsuited anymore to live in this one. She didn't understand that he was blaming her for keeping him on Earth and keeping

[7] MS *Wood*, Bodleian

him in his body. The man Elizabeth rescued from prison was abandoned by Heaven and by the deep revelations of his own heart. Augustine Baker didn't understand that he was the last in the line of great medieval mystics and that the love for Elizabeth which he had felt in his heart was the love of God for the Lady of the Laurel Hedge. He only knew that Heaven had cast him out and that his heart was empty, that there was a hole in it. The hole had to be there, but he didn't know that. He had a hole where the love of God should be, and he blamed Elizabeth for that.

No matter how hard the angels tried to explain it to Augustine Baker, he could not understood that God and the saints were no longer there, that they had fallen, (were in the process of falling, and would continue to fall for three hundred years), and that Baker's desire to be with them meant that he would have to fall too. Baker didn't understand this. He assumed that he was being turned away because he was unworthy of Paradise, and that he was unworthy because he was still attached too strongly to the things of the Earth and that this attachment was his love for Elizabeth. He thought that his desolation started at the exact moment when he had fallen in love. This was his mistake.

Elizabeth waited for Augustine Baker to return to her from prison. He never came. Let me be very clear about this: there is no written account of Elizabeth Fortesque in Augustine Baker's life. In everything that I've read I have found no record of Elizabeth Fortesque. But Baker told me this story many times while sitting on the leather wingback chair in my study looking through the french windows at the snow falling into the garden. He told it to me again in the stillness of the night. He said that he didn't go back to the Fortesque's garden to see Elizabeth, and that they never saw each other again. Elizabeth didn't marry, and because she had renounced her faith to rescue Baker, she couldn't go to Cambrai to join the Benedictine nuns-in-exile. She vowed that she would never enter the garden until she entered it with him. The garden for her had become the place of the sacred marriage. To enter alone meant nothing.

She started dressing entirely in black. She wandered from room to room in the house and stood before a window and looked out into the garden, or she opened the window slowly and then looked out. "Come to me. Come." she prayed over and over in her mind. But nobody came. She always prayed. And she always waited. She wandered from room to room, and she dreamed about the day when she would go out there again and be married in the sacred grove at the centre of her beloved garden.

5th Purport:

for Wilfrid Reeve

> "Fr Baker, if I mistake not,may rightly
> be regarded as the last of the line of
> great medieval mystics." Abbot Butler,
> *Downside Review XXX*, 1911.

Following is a partial list of books written by Augustine Baker for the nuns of Cambrai when he was their spiritual director, (1624 to 1633):

An Ideots Devotion *
A Spiritual Alphabet.
The Anchor of the Spirit
* ('An Ideots Devotion' also titled *The Holy Practices of a Divine Lover.*)

On the very first night that I ever slept with Claudette, (see Chapter 1), I told her, "I like to think I resemble the last great monk of the monastic period...", and she said, "I'm sure you resemble the very last great mystic of the monastic period."

Claudette had said "mystic" and I had said "monk", but my assumption had always been that both titles must belong to the same person. I soon discovered, however, that there is considerable disagreement about who was the last great monk and mystic, of the monastic period.

Augustine Baker was definitely a mystic, but there is some question whether or not he can be considered a "monk" at all since he rarely lived in a monastery with the Benedictines: he spent many years as a missionary on the English Mission, and was spiritual director of the nuns at Cambrai for nine years, then, when he did live with the monks at Douai, he was excused the usual duties of monastic life because of his health.

There was another monk who lived after Baker's time who was also considered an 'illuminant', and who lived a strict monastic life. This was Brother Lawrence, (1611-1691), a french lay monk of the Carmelite Order who is described as having attained "unclouded vision". [1]

However, the question of "who was the last great monk of the monastic period" is not one of dates, or of mode of life. Augustine Baker's greatness lies in his direct succession to the earliest medieval

---

[1] Cheney, *Men Who Have Walked With God.*

mystics. He can be seen as continuing a style of writing that is more in keeping with the style of Meister Eckhart or Julian of Norwich than with the English humanist writers of the Reformation, such as John Fisher or Thomas More.

In fact, it could be said that Augustine Baker studied directly with the earliest medieval mystics, and that their books were his true spiritual masters: "Since he never met a spiritual director who could help him personally, reading was his only guide to the mystical way."[2] The same scholar goes so far as to speculate that "[Baker] may have written treatises to the nuns of Cambrai when he was their spiritual adviser, instead of simply talking to them, because of the importance of the written word in his own spiritual development."[3]

That's how I decided that Baker was the last great monk of the monastic period: he loved language. The mystic's challenge is basically one of language. The challenge is to find a way of writing about an intimate experience of God in a linguistic system that, since the time of Philo of Alexandria, (and the combining of the Hellenic system of logic with the Hebraic tradition of literalism), required God to remain on the outside of it.

God, of course, is not really 'outside' language. He is 'immanent' with it: God cannot be contained within any idea of God, (God is greater than anything, therefore He is greater than any idea of Him), so God cannot be contained within language, but He is necessary for its functioning. He is the frame within which language is held. He is a linguistic necessity, the ultimate metaphor, and the hidden meaning in every text.

Language brings God into our lives, and then keeps Him away from us, at a little distance removed. God is the wall around the Garden of Eden and the margin that surrounds every text: He is transcendent because He is never in the text itself, but He is immanent because He is always on the same page.

When Claudette and I were in Europe in 1971 we spent a night in Douai, in Alsace, where Augustine Baker had been in exile with the other English Benedictine monks at the monastery of St Gregory. Since the 17th Century the town of Douai has been destroyed three times, first in the French Revolution, and then in World War I and World War II. Today nothing remains of the English Benedictine structures.

---

[2] Anthony Low, *Augustine Baker.*

[3] ibid.

Then Claudette and I crossed the Channel to England and spent two days in Oxford where I found a copy of *The Life of Augustine Baker* by Wilfrid Reeve, in the Duke Humphrey's Library at the Bodleian. It was one of twenty-two hand-written copies completed by Reeve between 1677 and 1690 as part of a manuscript campaign to support a movement for Baker's canonization.

Then, using the details I found in Reeve's *Life*, Claudette and I drove to the small town of Cadbury in the County of Devonshire and had afternoon tea at the Fersden Estate, which is now open to the public. This was the place where Augustine Baker had experienced his third conversion and had dismissed the Lady of the Laurel Hedge as a temptation of the devil. Then we stopped the car just outside the village of Cadbury on the hill overlooking the road to Tiverton. A figure was walking on the road in the distance. We could see for miles. The clouds were so low and the hill was so high we thought we could take one step forward and be in heaven.

Augustine Baker is known for his significant contribution to the history of English mysticism, and he is also known for the lack of clarity in his style of writing[f]. He wanders here and there and does not come to any definite point. I like this fault. It reminds me of walking in a garden in early morning.

You might say that Baker's writing was too heavily influenced by the attitude of the gardener, and not sufficiently influenced by the attitude of the landscape architect. He did not seem to know where to stand on the surrounding wall in order to see the garden in perspective. His writing had no symmetry.

Justin McCann, a Baker scholar and Benedictine monk, stated the same fact this way: "[Baker's] books are, in fact, constructed by the method of addition, rather than on a formal plan with beginning, middle and end, so that they tend to be invertebrate".

I have spent many hours sitting in my study talking with Augustine Baker about his life and about gardening and about writing, and we both came to the same conclusion: back then, when he was writing treatises to the nuns at Cambrai, he was angry with perspective, and it was this anger which gave his writing its lack of form. At first it was clear that Baker's anger was directed at the angels of God for keeping him out of heaven and leaving him kneeling in the fertilized soil to hack away at the things that needed taking out. But then it became clear that

[f] David Knowles emphasises this point in *The English Mystical Tradition*, comparing Baker unfavourably to both Teresa of Avila and the author of *The Cloud* in terms of clarity.

he was also angry with the Lady of the Laurel Hedge for holding him here when he wanted to leave. Our final conclusion was that Baker was suspended between Heaven and Earth, unable to live totally in either place.

"You must be tired of hovering between these two worlds", I said, "I mean, you're neither on the margin nor in the text."

"What I have learned," Baker said, "is that the solution is not to choose one over the other, but to find a way to be in both at once."

We agreed that this is also the constant tension in language, and that this is the problem that faces every reader, and that whenever we turn a page we are confronted by it: how can we be in the text and outside it at the same time? For instance, when I described stopping the car on a hill in Devonshire near the village of Cadbury overlooking the road to Tiverton, and said that we could see for miles — (oh, I love talking about that view! the clouds moved gently towards us from a far distance in a blue, blue sky, and the shadows of those clouds followed the contour of the landscape from field to field, while the breeze made great swirling patterns across the tops of the grain, the sun shone, cattle grazed, and a figure passed in and out of the shadows of the clouds as he walked into the distance along the road to Tiverton) — when you read that, were you on the margin or in the text? Were you in my position and Claudette's on top of the hill, or were you the figure walking on the road in the distance? Or were you somewhere else entirely on another hill in another part of England? Or was your mind far away beyond the horizon where they have no margins and no page, and where the book is a simple thing made by those who make stone fences: the words are lifted into place one at a time, and the book is written in a thousand years. Were you there? Were you able to read the text in that book?

Then tell me that it's true, that the writing in the great book is just the motion of the shadows cast by clouds as they drift high in the sky, high above a rambling sentence that describes a man walking into the far distance on a road that leads to Tiverton.

Chapter 9

> "... take thee but a little word of one
> syllable, for it is better than of two, for
> ever the shorter it is the better. And
> such a word is this word God or this
> word Love. With this word thou shalt
> beat on this cloud and this darkness
> above thee. With this word thou shalt
> smite down all manner of thought
> under the cloud of forgetting."
> *The Cloud of Unknowing*, (Chapter 6).

I fell in love with Claudette all over again on the day she came back to my house to visit the garden, the day on which we discovered the new shoot of Tante Hugette's rosebush. She was dressed entirely in black. We sat at the kitchen table until midnight talking and drinking two bottles of wine. Then we both looked at the little clock above the stove, then we looked at each other, and it was midnight. It's utterly different falling in love when you're older. In fact, you don't fall in love at all, you simply turn your head and see the little clock above the stove, realize it's midnight, then look into her eyes and recognize her for the first time.

I got up from the table and said to Claudette: "I know who you are. And I know what's happening to you". I went to my study and came back carrying a bottle of brandy in one hand and a copy of the *Egyptian Book of the Dead* in the other. I opened the *Egyptian Book of the Dead*, (as compiled by Wallis Budge, Citadel Press, New Jersey), to a representation of the gesture that the Lady in Black had been making while she stood at the edge of the St Lawrence River at sunrise in Old Montreal and struck her forehead repeatedly with the palm of her open hand. I pointed to the picture and explained that the Lady was making the mantric sign of *Sorrow*, and that this was telling Claudette that the Lady was associated with the work of Isis, the work of retrieving her masculine element, the god Osiris, from the Underworld. I told Claudette how the goddess Isis spent a lifetime travelling all over Egypt gathering together the pieces of her dismembered Osiris until he was whole again. Then I explained that the name the Lady kept repeating over and over in Claudette's mind had to be the name of Claudette's own particular Osiris.

"Quite simply", I said, "you are being initiated into the rites of Isis."

Claudette nodded her head. "You're right. And I've been trying to tell you this all night: I have already met my Osiris. I met him at the Meditation Centre on Pine Avenue on Mount Royal. I went there after the Lady in Black almost pushed me into the river. Osiris is my beloved, and he is a man you know."

Claudette had gone to the Meditation Centre at the invitation of one of the art critics she met at the opening night party for the exhibition of her seven new canvases which she called *The Seven Sorrows*. She went to the Meditation Centre as a desperate attempt to reconnect with the spiritual direction of Tante Huguette after the Lady in Black tried to kill her. She said, "I thought maybe Tante Huguette wanted me to take up the Eastern spiritual practice of the mantra."

That is not what happened. The Meditation Centre on Pine Avenue turned out to be the Benedictine Priory of Montreal. It was run by a group of Benedictine monks from England. The form of prayer that these Christian monks were teaching was identical to the mantra known in Eastern spiritual tradition, but was, in fact, a Christian form of the mantra rooted in the practices of the Desert Fathers who lived in Egypt in the first four centuries of Christianity. The "imageless prayer" that the monks were teaching in Montreal was the same formula for prayer that had been taught to Saint Cassian by Abba Issac in the deserts of Egypt in 419 A.D., and which Cassian later described in The Conferences. [1]

The man who directed the Benedictine Priory in Montreal was Father John Main. He was the man who reintroduced the mantra, (in 1975 at Ealing Abbey in England), to the Benedictine Order as a form of Christian prayer. John Main had spent years searching for an historical precedent, a justification in Church history, for the mantra. He loved this form of prayer but had been ordered to give it up when he joined the Benedictine Order in 1959.

John Main was the man who introduced Claudette to her Osiris. When he talked briefly before the meditation, he said that the specific mantra he suggested for everyone was the phrase "Maranatha". He explained that this was an Aramaic phrase, the language that Jesus himself spoke, and meant "Come, Lord Jesus". He said: "St Paul ends Corinthians with it, and John ends Revelation with it. It is probably the most ancient prayer in the Church." [2]

---

[1] See the *Second Conference of Abba Issac on Prayer.*

[2] *In the Stillness Dancing* (The Journey of John Main), Neil McKenty, p85.

After the meditation Claudette introduced herself to John Main, and she had tears in her eyes. She took his hand and said only "thank you." She felt grateful to him for having introduced her to her Osiris. This is how John Main did that: in his introduction he said that he began his search for the Christian roots to the mantra after reading the book "Sancta Sophia", (Holy Wisdom), by the 17th Century Benedictine illuminant Augustine Baker.

"Baker's frequent reminder of the emphatic insistence St Benedict places upon Cassian's *Conferences* sent me to them seriously for the first time," he said. "In Baker's writing there is an instinctive understanding of the mantra." [3]

Hearing the name of Augustine Baker was Claudette's third crisis. She became upset for a moment, and then she became completely calm when she realized that the voice inside her had become calm. She realized that the Lady in Black had been leading her to this place all along, that Tante Huguette had left her the minute the rosebush had been taken from the garden and that the Lady in Black had emerged from the hole left there. She had come to guide Claudette into the darkness of that hole.

She realized that the phrase which the Lady in Black had been repeating over and over in her mind was the same phrase that John Maine had just taught her.

Her third crisis occurred when she realized that everything that had happened to her was still connected with me, that somehow our relationship wasn't over yet. She said: "It's like you say, it's been a journey of Isis. I was led away from you and back to the Gaspé and then to the Benedictine Priory in Montreal, (which is the former McConnell mansion on Mount Royal overlooking the St Lawrence River and the woods of Vermont in the far distance - there's a spectacular view from there in the Fall), only to meet my Osiris who is none other than your Augustine Baker."

As Claudette spoke I felt two powerful and contradictory feelings: on the one hand I was deeply relieved that she had not fallen in love with someone new, but on the other hand I was greatly troubled that she was taking Augustine Baker away from me. Then I thought something worse, something much worse: I thought that maybe everything that had happened to me since I dug the rosebush out of the garden was for Claudette's benefit. I started thinking that maybe I had gone to the threshold of Heaven and had suffered my year of Emptiness lying on

[3] ibid.

bare rock under grey skies outside the gates of paradise, only so I could tell Claudette all about Heaven being empty and about an axis that now passes between Heaven and the depth of the Earth, just so she could understand how he had come to her, her beloved Augustine Baker.

Then Claudette told me something that made me relax. She said: "My falling into the St Lawrence River was meant to be a symbolic falling. Where I needed to fall, really, was to the depth of myself, to the depth of sorrow that the Lady in Black was opening for me. I had to follow her down the hole left by the rosebush. I had to stand at the perimeter of the sacred Grove of the Mothers of Quebec. That's where I went: I went to a place deep inside myself and stood at the edge of a Grove and saw all the Mothers standing in a circle, while, in the middle of the circle a seated Lady kept repeating over and over the phrase "Maranatha". And that's where I've been all winter, deep inside myself, standing at the edge of the Grove with my own mother and her mother's mother and all our mothers before them. And I felt with them the salt embrace of all the years of separation from the Beloved. Women have always taken care of the serious business of life while the men have always gone off somewhere. They have gone off to sea, or off to war, or off to heaven leaving us alone and exposed for centuries on the rock-formation at the base of ourselves. I stood at the edge of the sacred Grove and prayed "Maranatha" with the mothers. This was more sorrowful for me than visiting the Gaspé. It was more sorrowful than Egypt must have been for Isis. The Grove was like the place where the St Lawrence and the Nile meet each other and flow together into the sea forever."

Claudette told me this while we were still sitting across from each other at the kitchen table. Essentially, she was telling me that while I had gone to the gates of Heaven, she had gone to the opposite end of the axis that joins Heaven to the depth of the Earth. Then she said:

"The Lady in Black told me to come and visit you today. She said that there was something you had discovered in your research on the life of Augustine Baker about a woman who died with something unresolved with him. That's who the Lady in Black is. She is that woman. So tell me about her: is she one of the nuns at Cambrai when Baker was their spiritual director, or was she a woman he knew while on the English Mission? Whoever she is, she is someone he abandoned, someone he hurt very deeply".

We went upstairs to the antechamber of the bedroom. I started a fire in the fireplace and Claudette went to take a bath. She said she missed the luxury of our double-size bathtub because she had only a shower stall in her tiny studio/apartment in Montreal. When she came back she was wearing a silk kimono. Her hair was up and her body was powdered and perfumed, and as she came into the room she let down her hair. On the table beside the brandy was a pitcher of distilled water. I filled two tumblers with water and handed one of the tumblers to Claudette, then sat back and told her the entire story of Elizabeth Fortesque as told to me by Augustine Baker in my study and in the quiet of my bedroom in the middle of the night. I described the scene of Elizabeth waiting in the garden for Baker to come back to her after she had rescued him from prison. I explained how this event was the beginning of Baker's "great desolation" which lasted until he met the Lady of the Laurel Hedge in another garden in another part of England near the village of Cadbury in the county of Devonshire where Claudette and I went for afternoon tea three hundred years later. I described the confusion that Elizabeth felt when Baker didn't come, and the sorrow she felt now that she was without God and without the man for whom she had renounced God. I can remember the specific words I used to end my story: "And so, she started dressing entirely in black, and the stillness of her garden was never broken by his footsteps again."

As I told the story Claudette tucked her knees up on the seat of the chair and rocked back and forth. She rocked back and forth and looked into the fire.

I said: "Maybe you are bringing Augustine Baker and Elizabeth Fortesque together again. Maybe they need to meet in my garden, and that's why you came here today."

Claudette kept rocking and looking into the fire. I told her that her story had shaken my confidence, that I wasn't certain anymore about the nature of my connection to Augustine Baker. "You need to understand something," I said, "I have not been able to authenticate the episode of Elizabeth Fortesque in any of my reading on Baker's life. Baker himself told me the story while we sat in my study watching the snow fall into the walled garden, but I'm not sure now if Augustine Baker created Elizabeth Fortesque simply as an image of his inner conflict with the feminine, or whether I created both Elizabeth and Baker as images of my inner conflicts. I suppose that Baker is a metaphor for me, a metaphor that creates a bridge between me and the light of heaven."

Claudette kept her eyes on the fire and said: "You're wrong. Augustine Baker is my bridge to the light of heaven. I mean, it was Augustine Baker who led John Main back to Saint Cassian who then led John Main to Egypt where he learned a mantra from the Desert Fathers. Then I learned the mantra from him - from John Main - and this is the same mantra that the Lady in the sacred Grove repeats over and over. I say it every day now. It is my new spiritual practice. Your bridge is Tante Huguette. And she is your bridge to the light in matter. She has fallen all the way from heaven into your walled garden just to give you a new daily practice, which, of course, is gardening. Gardening will teach you everything you need to know about the light in matter."

I said: "Why does everybody think I am the gardener?" I shook my head. "Besides, I know everything I need to know about the light in matter. I've been learning about it all winter. The light in matter is only something reflected from the light of heaven. There is no light in matter itself."

"You're wrong about that." she said. "There is a light in matter but it throws shadows. Don't be confused by the shadows." Then Claudette stood up and stretched slowly. She was standing between me and the light of the fire and I could see the shadow of her body through her silk kimono. She said she was ready for bed, but we didn't make it to the bedroom. We made love right there on the Persian carpet in front of the fire. Then we went to bed.

There was a storm that night and the shadows of the branches of the linden were wild on the bedroom window blinds. The storm woke me, and Claudette and I made love again. Afterwards I turned on the bedside light so I could look at Claudette's body, and when I got up from the bed I noticed that the bedside light was now behind me and that I was looking at Claudette's body in the shadow of my body. Then, when I carried the tray of ice water into the bedroom from the antechamber, I looked at Claudette's body and the light of the bedside lamp was between us shining in my eyes and all I could see was the light itself and, behind the light, the shadow of Claudette's body huge on the wall. I said: "You should see yourself". She said: "Turn around." And my own shadow was huge on the blinds of the bedroom window. Then my shadow moved suddenly across the ceiling toward the shadow of Claudette's outstretched arms, and our shadows met and overlapped and grew darker than the storm outside, darker than the centre of the storm, darker than the darkness that had entered Claudette's paintings, and darker than the things that were climbing the linden and hanging from the limbs and breaking off branches and throwing them to the ground and swinging back and forth against the window and calling like the wind or like a linden that creaks in the shadows moved by the wind.

That's where I found my love for Claudette, in the place where our shadows overlapped, in the darkest part of the dark.

6th Purport

As I made love to Claudette that night, I fell completely in love. I realize that I have mentioned this fact already, (and I certainly don't want to labour it), but I need to clarify one point: I didn't fall in love with Claudette. I fell in love with the Lady to whom Claudette led me during our love-making. You see, as I was making love to Claudette, (in fact, at the precise moment when we reached the peak of our passion), I experienced a profound connection to the Lady of the Rose. I felt utterly close to Her and knew that She had been with me already and always. I realized that I had been devoted to Her all my life and that I had gone looking for Her in all the cathedrals and galleries of Europe and at every road-side shrine that I passed along the way.

This is what happened:

As I was making love to Claudette I experienced myself falling into the darkest part of the dark. I felt that I was falling and falling down a tunnel. This tunnel is the axis that is passing through the centre of the novel, the axis that joins Heaven and Earth together and passes through the hole in my heart. Then, finally, I felt that I was at the bottom of the tunnel, and then I saw the Lady of the Rose. I saw Her seated in a grove of laurels. She looked exactly the same as when She came into my garden earlier that day leaving behind a shoot of Tante Huguette's rosebush. She looked exactly like Our Lady of Perugia. She looked exactly like the seated Lady of the Rose who had saved my life when I was ten. She was all the Ladies I had ever loved. I wanted to reach out and hold Her in my arms, so I stepped into the grove of laurels and the Lady said: "I have been with you forever. But if you approach me now you must be prepared to die."

I was startled that she wanted me to die and I hesitated, and in that moment of hesitation I felt a pain in my back and I heard Claudette speak my name once, then twice, then three times. We were at the climax of our love-making and she was digging her fingernails into my upper back and shoulders. I heard my own voice calling out. I heard myself calling out to the Lady. In fact, I think I was shouting. I was shouting my love for Her. Then, suddenly, I was in the bedroom again rolling onto my back next to Claudette. Tears were in my eyes and I was breathing heavily.

Claudette too was breathing heavily. She raised herself onto one elbow and said: "Are you alright?" I nodded my head, and Claudette told me that she had just had the most profound experience just now during our love-making. She said: "He came to me. It was really him. Really. First I saw you, then I saw John Main, and then I saw Him! Augustine Baker, and then you and John Main were contained in Augustine Baker and he was like a light shining. He went down on one knee before me, and then he kissed my hand, and as he kissed my hand I could see on my sleeve that I was wearing black, and I realized that he was speaking to me as Elizabeth Fortesque, and his eyes filled with tears and he asked my forgiveness, and I said "Yes, my love; of course, my love", and we held each other and it was wonderful between us. He was here just now. Really, it was him."

Then Claudette fell back and fell asleep. She fell into a deep, deep sleep. That's when I got out of bed and went into the garden and wept my prayer of love to the Lady. I stood in the middle of the walled garden, (in the middle of the night, in the middle of the storm), and turned toward the place where the Lady of the Rose had appeared naked earlier that day, and said:

"Alright, alright, I am the gardener! I promise to care for the rose-shoot you sent into my garden today. I will do this because you love me, because you have loved me all my life, when no one else loved me. I remember how you loved me when I was ten, admiring the weight of my head in your lap and the warmth of my face of your skin and the endless dedication of my mouth on your nipple.

"I remember, and now I come to you as Gabriel. "I come as the messenger for Him, Himself, the One. I accept that He is your true lover and that I am only the messenger. He is coming right behind me into your garden, your garden that will soon be fluttering with blossoms on a breeze, your garden that will flutter for Him, Him who is the breeze, Him who descends on a breeze like a dove, Him who is the dove, Him whose heart will mingle with you among the blossoms and among all the secret meanings hidden among the blossoms and in their scent, meanings that are lovers' secrets that only you two share, secrets that mingle and flutter in a walled garden that is a symbol for your love, a symbol for this fluttering heart prepared for you, this fluttering heart of Gabriel."

Then I went back to bed, and in the morning Claudette was gone. In fact, all that was left of the night was a backyard littered with branches that had blown down in the storm, and a letter from Claudette propped against a wine glass beside an empty bottle of 1970 Bordeaux in the middle of the kitchen table.

Chapter 10:
Part I

> "It was presumed by the Fathers and
> early commentators on Scripture, that
> the Annunciation must have taken place
> in springtime at eventide soon after
> sunset."
> (*Legends of the Madonna*, Anna Jameson)

The next morning when I sat down at the kitchen table to read
Claudette's letter I felt awful. Claudette was gone and I was alone in the
house for the second time. I opened the envelope and read the letter. I
read it twice. Then I put down the letter and looked at the sun shining
through the kitchen window. I watched the dust particles move in the
light for a long time, and then I read the letter again. I found myself
underlining the important parts. This is a habit I had developed over the
years from reading so many manuscripts and essays. I can hardly read
anything anymore without underlining it. Then I stood up and walked
back and forth between the kitchen table and the stove. Then I picked up
the letter again, then I threw it down and grabbed the pencil from the
table and broke it in two and threw the pieces across the room and
slammed the kitchen door as I went into the backyard and started picking
up the fallen branches from the ground. I started beside the new rose
shoot. Augustine Baker came walking over to me from his customary
place on the love-seat and stood directly behind me. He said that the broken branches of the linden in my hand looked like the antlers of a stag. I
told him I didn't feel like talking right now. Then he did something
unusual. He placed a hand on my shoulder, and said: "Your time is
come. All is well. Today you meet her."

Baker had never touched me before. Immediately I placed my
own hand on top of his hand and turned to look at him. In the same
moment a woman's voice in front of me said: "I forbid you to be here in
my garden!"

Without looking at her I said: "I am the new gardener. This is
not your garden anymore."

"And my roses, where are my roses? What have you done to the
roses of Our Lady?" I turned and saw that the woman I was talking to
was not Claudette. Already I had forgotten that Claudette had left for
Montreal after spending a wonderful night with me. Claudette herself
described our night together as wonderful. She used that exact word in

the letter she left on the kitchen table. I remember specifically underlining the word wonderful. She also said that she didn't want to see me again until the end of summer. She said she needed to be alone with the experience of last night, the experience of being "embraced by Augustine Baker in the grove of the Mothers" until it became her own experience utterly and not something that depended on me for its recurrence. This is the way she put it: "I cannot expect you to be my bridge to the sacred grove. The grove is a place inside me, and I must know that I can go there anytime by myself, and for myself."

That was another part of the letter that I had found myself underlining a few minutes ago. The Lady talking to me in the garden looked fierce and terrible. She was haggard and thin like something carved from the wood of a poplar tree.

"What have you done to the roses of Our Lady?" she said.

I felt Augustine Baker's hand squeezing my shoulder. "Your roses are dead, dear Lady," I said.

"Nothing associated with me or my name ever dies." she said.

"They are dead." I said.

The Lady raised her arms and shook herself in a fury. A strong wind blew storm clouds into the garden. The Lady was dressed in the habit of a nun except that the head-veil was missing.

Her skin was pale and her hair was short and ragged and laced with branches of the laurel. Instead of a crucifix around her neck she wore a string of rosary beads made from large pieces of ivory or bone. As she shook herself and raised her arms, the beads rolled back and forth against her chest and I could see that each bead was carved with two faces. One face was the face of Mary (of *The Seven Sorrows*), and the other face was the face of a skull. The storm clouds grew darker. The Lady was the darkness. And the storm.

"I never die, I tell you. I live on and on and carve the image of my suffering into the world, the suffering of all women who have been spurned by the beloved, all women whose precious gift has been rejected."

"But who are you, and what do you want from me?"

"I am Tante Huguette." she said. "I am She, the aunt of the woman you know as Claudette. And if you wish to stay in my garden, you must be prepared to die."

Chapter 10:
Part II

> "God chose to let our redemption depend
> upon the consent of this young girl."
> (Commentary on the First Joyful Mystery
> of the Rosary, the Annunciation.) Maisie
> Ward, *The Splendor of the Rosary*.

The only part of Claudette's letter which I underlined twice was the part where she described in more detail what she saw during our lovemaking. As you will remember from the 6th Purport, Claudette first saw an image of me, then she saw an image of John Main, and then she saw Augustine Baker, and then both John Main and I were contained in Baker who was like a light shining. The part that I underlined twice was the following sentences in which Claudette realized that this sequence of images signified the completion of her initiation into the rites of Isis: "... you, and John Main, and Augustine Baker all became one. [I realized that] ... you were contained in Him. You became an aspect of Baker who is my Osiris. [Therefore] ... all the pieces of Osiris are together again. They are together now in my heart. He is whole. He is one."

So, it was very clear: Claudette was in love with Augustine Baker, and Augustine Baker was treating her like the Lady in Black, Elizabeth Fortesque herself. And I was just the bridge they crossed to get to each other. My own bridge was Tante Huguette. She was my bridge to the Lady of the Rose.

Tante Huguette stood before me in the walled garden, looking old and ravaged and full of grief. I said to her: "You have fallen from heaven to bring me an important message of the greatest urgency. You must tell it to me, for today the Lady of the Rose is coming into my garden."

Tante Huguette laughed a deep and throaty laugh full of implications of a vast and dangerous knowledge. She said: "You are waiting for me: I serve the Lady of the Rose. And I have never, ever, been to heaven."

Chapter 10:
Part III

> And Mary said: "be it done unto me
> according to thy word."
> *Luke 1: 38*

Tante Huguette's voice was the sound of branches that move violently against a window in a wind, and her laugh was the branches snapping. I had thought that the Lady of the Rose would come Herself in response to my prayer. I had imagined Her coming into my garden with Her missing arm restored making a gesture that would be familiar to me and which would complete the life-long bonding process between us. Instead Tante Huguette arrived with her pale skin and piercing eyes and hair like laurel branches without blooms.

"When I died I didn't go to heaven." she said. "I went to Rimouski." She laughed. "God threw me out of heaven. He rejected me! And He rejected my roses! He took away my life of creativity and made me care for the little children, my baby sisters, and then He kept me out of heaven because I could not love those children. I have been mocked by the sparkling diamond face of God, so I have made His children tend my roses, my beautiful roses that have stopped blooming and never will bloom again forever now."

Then Tante Huguette took hold of the beads around her neck and moved her fingers from bead to bead as if counting the injustices done to her by God.

"God kept me from my life, from the roses of my creativity. I wanted to be an artist and teacher, but the babies cried and they cried because God took my mother away and left me with all the babies! How I raged at Him. How I raged at Him for taking away my mother. But then I was rescued by the great Mother Herself, and I became part of Her, I became part of the Great Mother who seeks revenge. I have carved the beads of Her rosary with my own hands in memory of my dead roses. I cry for my roses, and I leave the children to suck from the breasts of all the dead mothers."

I wanted to get out of the garden and into the house and close the windows and doors. Tante Huguette took pride in the way she kept the three youngest children close to her after she died. She explained that she hovered near them when they were still young and then, when they were old enough to leave home, she gave them each a roseplant to remember her by. She made them tend the roses of her creativity that wouldn't bloom for her. She made them pay for the injustice done to her by Him. She made them live the life she couldn't live. She said: "I gave them each a rosebush for their gardens, and when they planted my roses they planted my dreams."

When Tante Huguette finished her litany she stopped fingering her rosary. Augustine Baker took his hand away from my shoulder in the same moment. He moved onto the wall behind the lilac bush. He stood on the wall looking like a light shining through the storm that Tante Huguette had brought with her into the garden. I was alone on my knees in front of this Lady who had danced upward from the bottom of the hole where the rosebush used to be.

Tante Huguette said: "Now you know who I am. But who are you, and what are you doing in this garden without roses?" I was still holding the broken branches of the linden in my left hand. Automatically I put my right hand over my heart and held the linden branches out to Tante Huguette:

"I am the Archangel Gabriel." I said. "I bring you a message from the sparkling diamond face of God."

"I will never look on that face again!" she said. "I have been spurned by Him and I will never love Him again!"

"He wants to be forgiven." I said. Tante Huguette's face filled with surprise and she looked around the garden for the first time. Her expression was one of wonder, as if all the flowering plants and shrubs had come into bloom at once, as if the lilac flowered next to the rose of sharon, as if maple seeds swirled downward on a breeze, and the blossoms of the bridle-wreath spirea fluttered in the air among the blooms of the white hydrangea. Tante Huguette turned to me: "Are we in Persia?" she said, as if a morning dove or nightingale had just called from beyond the far corner of the garden wall, "or is this a painting of the *Assumption of Mary Into Heaven*?"

"No." I said. "This is a painting of *the Annunciation*."

Tante Huguette shook herself and the sky grew dark again. She looked deeply hurt and very sad. "It has been a long time! How can I forgive Him when He has been so cruel?"

"He is waiting on the garden wall for your answer." I said. "He is waiting to see if your roses will bloom again." Tante Huguette was completely silent now. A profound calm filled the garden. Then she said: "He kept me waiting, now let Him wait."

And Augustine Baker waited for three days. That's how long my meeting with Tante Huguette lasted. Over and over again I listened to the litany of grievances that she had against God. However, by the end of our meeting I had managed to arrange the marriage between Augustine Baker and the Lady of the Rose. I completed the arrangements by fulfilling a list of specific requirements set out by Tante Huguette. The requirements involved major design changes to the garden. It took me seven months to finish everything. The wedding took place on the last day of October on the eve of the feast of All Saints. Claudette was there and she cried. The garden was more beautiful than she could have imagined.

That was the night when the Lady of the Rose entered paradise. She wasn't taken up to Heaven — she brought Heaven to Earth — and Augustine Baker came down from the wall wearing a crown of laurels. And they were married right there, at the centre of my walled garden.

Chapter 10:
Part IV

> "Saint Bernard says that [Mary] was
> studying the book of Isaiah, and as she
> recited the verse, "Behold, a Virgin
> shall conceive and bear a son," she
> thought within her heart in great
> humility, "How blessed the woman of
> whom these words are written! Would I
> might be but her handmaid to serve
> her...!" - when, in the same instant, the
> wondrous vision burst upon her, and the
> holy prophesy was realized in herself."
> *Legends of the Madonna*, Anna Jameson.

This chapter tells the story of how Tante Huguette was betrayed by God in the last year of her life. It tells of how she was then rejected by Him after her death, and of how this made her a handmaid to the Lady of the Rose.

When Tante Huguette came home to the Gaspé for her mother's funeral she had no intention of staying in Rimouski to take care of her baby sisters who had no mother because she had just died. Huguette was twenty years old, and she fully intended to return to her convent in Montreal, (the convent of Notre Dame de Bon Secours, founded by Marguerite Bourgeoys), where Huguette would take her final vows, and become a teacher, and continue her life of painting. Great pressure was put on Huguette by her family however, and by the monseigneur at the church, to become the new substitute mother to the children. But she refused, and refused, and refused, until she received a letter from her order in Montreal saying that they understood, (after receiving communications from concerned parties in Rimouski), that Huguette's family needed her more than the order needed her and that her place was with the little babies. She cried every night. She cried for herself and for all her unfinished paintings. She was trapped in Rimouski forever.

"Whenever I looked at my little baby sisters I hated them, but whenever I felt the hate rising I managed to choke it back because I knew the babies were innocent. Then the choking became a cough, and the cough became a cold, and the cold became consumption, and I returned to Montreal where I did my final series of paintings of Mary and made a good death."

Tante Huguette told me this story many times. She also told me the following story many times, the story of what happened to her after she died and was turned away from the gates of heaven.

"I made a very good death." she said. "I prayed and I prayed to Mary right until the final moment of my life. Then, suddenly, I rose higher and higher on a cloud toward heaven, but when I got to the gates of Paradise I was told I must go back. I felt so ashamed. I was ashamed of having thought I was worthy of Paradise in the first place, ashamed because I knew God was angry with me for having abandoned the children, and because I had chosen to die rather than give up my life of painting. I was sure that He must hate all artists because we are so selfish. Then I turned around and looked back at the Earth and I could see the shoreline of the Gaspé peninsula. Standing there on the Gaspé - in fact, standing right in the middle of the backyard of my family home in Rimouski - was a Lady with Her arms held open to me. I could see from Her eyes that She understood everything that I was feeling in that moment of rejection, and I fell to Her. I fell and I fell, and when I reached Her arms She held me tight. She didn't smile. She never smiles. She looks fierce and dark and full of power and I have never seen anything like Her in all the paintings of all the Madonnas in the entire history of Western Art. Her heart is a beautiful rosebush that has stopped blooming. She calls Herself *the Lady Pierced in the Heart by Thorns.*"

"All the angels of heaven have fallen to Earth." I said. "They are Gabriels kneeling awkwardly in gardens, they are nightingales singing their longing for paradise from poplar boughs that overhang garden gates."

"Don't be ridiculous." She said. "Nobody sings love songs to *The Lady Pierced in the Heart by Thorns*. She has been spurned and rejected and I have joined Her. I promised to make Her roses bloom again. I promised that I would never let my own roses fade, the roses I planted in the summer before my death. So I went back to Rimouski and made the three youngest children take care of them, and even when the children left home I gave them each a cutting of my rosebush which they planted in their own gardens. Claudette's mother was the only one of the three children who remained devoted to my roses. The others forgot me. But Claudette's mother didn't forget and Claudette didn't forget. Claudette became my favourite. She was wonderful. She had more talent as a painter than I ever had, but now even she is gone from my garden and all the roses are dead."

"The old roses are dead", I said, "but a new rose has entered the garden, and I am here to tend it. You must listen to me. You must listen to the song of this nightingale, to the words of this humble Gabriel."

Tante Huguette shook herself in a fury again: "You are not the Archangel Gabriel!" she said. "In fact, you don't even look like one of the minor angels who attend Gabriel in the great paintings of *the Annunciation* or *the Assumption*."

"Well, I have been kneeling here a long time." I said. "In fact I have been kneeling in this position for five hundred years. You see, I am the Archangel Gabriel who Fra Angelico brought to Earth for his fresco of *The Annunciation* at the monastery of San Marco in Florence. But now it is time for me to move again. It is time for me to complete the work I started in Italy in the 15th Century."

"You have the nose of Fra Angelico's Gabriel," she said, "but in neither of the frescoes of *The Annunciation* that he completed at San Marco did he portray Gabriel holding dead branches, certainly not branches of the linden."

"They should be lilies." I said.

"You don't know as much about the Italian Renaissance as you think," she said, "because if those branches were lilies then you would be the Archangel Gabriel of the other artist monk, Fra Filippo Lippi. I much prefer him to Angelico. Filippo Lippi was a great painter. He loved showing Gabriel with flowers. With lilies. He was a far greater artist than Fra Angelico."

"You are horribly mistaken, madame. I have seen Filippo Lippi's fresco of *The Annunciation* at Spoleto Cathedral, and his Gabriel does not surpass Angelico's Gabriel. It comes close, but most Art historians consider it a copy."

"I'm not talking about his *Gabriel*!" she said. "It's Filippo Lippi's portrayals of *Mary* that account for his greatness. His Marys are real, and they have depth and feeling, unlike Angelico's, and Filippo Lippi shows Mary the way She really is, the way She appeared to me when She held out Her arms and I fell to Her from the gates of heaven."

"No! No! No!" I said. "Filippo Lippi was rude and selfish and vain, and his life was scandalous! His model for the Virgin in the Spoleto *Annunciation* was an innocent young woman named Lucrezia Buti. She was a nun, and Filippo Lippi fell in love with her while doing the fresco. He kidnapped her from her convent at Prato and took her to live with him in Venice where they had two children together. He betrayed the spirit of purity that had entered the Renaissance with Fra Angelico. But of course even the Church forgave him everything because he was a great painter."

"You are such a fool!" she said. "Fra Angelico painted the Virgin Mary. Filippo Lippi painted the real Mary. I don't care about the

Virgin! Don't you realize who I've been talking about? The Lady who opened Her arms to me was the Magdelaine, Mary Magdelaine , the true Lady of the Rose who has been rejected from the hearts of men for two thousand years."

"You misguided old witch!" I said. "The Lady you saw when you fell from heaven was not the Magdelaine, she was the Lady of Perugia, who is another form of the Lady of the Rose. I saw Her myself. She wore a long cape of the deepest blue and she was missing Her left arm at the elbow. She weeps endlessly for all of us who suffer."

"The Lady is wounded," she said, "but Her wound is in Her *heart*. She is not the Lady of Perugia because She has never been represented in any painting that I have ever seen. I told you that. Don't you angels ever listen! She is the forgotten and unforgiven aspect of Mother Mary. She has been driven underground since the beginning of Christianity. She has been forgotten and all men fear Her. You fallen angels think you know everything! But when you fall in love with the Virgin in your high-minded spiritual way, you get the Magdelaine as well, and the Magdelaine demands relationship, and you cannot relate to Her strength and power, so you run back to heaven. Heaven is filled with cowards like you. The Lady has been hurt so much by heaven! She hides in the darkest part of the dark. She is the shadow cast by the swaying linden in night storms. She is the thorn of the laurel that sticks in the flesh of men. I speak with Her voice and when you hear me you tremble."

"Just listen to you! Just listen to you." I said. "You are so utterly misguided. Everything you've said is based on a false premise. Your bitterness about Heaven and your manipulation of the children has been a selfish waste. You fell from Heaven because Heaven is closed. You were turned away from the gates because *everybody* is being turned away. God isn't there anymore. He has fallen to Earth in love, and in fact, I believe He has fallen in love with your *Lady Pierced in the Heart by Thorns*. Furthermore, the old roses of this garden died, not because God rejected them, but because the Lady herself doesn't want them anymore. She wants you to look up into the sparkling diamond face of God and open your arms to Him as He falls. And He is falling right now, right here into this garden."

Tante Huguette looked into the sky and saw nothing falling. She said: "As a girl I prayed on the rosary every day and I prayed that the Lady would guide me on the path to Her. Then one day it happened: I had a vision of Her. I was thirteen. I was praying on the rosary while sitting in the sun in the backyard of our house in Rimouski, I was on the exact spot where I planted my rosebush several years later, and I had this vision in which I saw a grove of trees surrounding a sunken garden, and Our Lady was sitting in the sunken garden beside a rosebush. She was surrounded by a circle of women, Her ladies-in-waiting. I knew I was in a secret place. Then, just as suddenly as it started, the vision began to fade, but in the last instant Our Lady turned to me and beckoned me with Her eyes, and that's when I decided to become a nun, and that's why I planted the rosebush on that spot when I knew I was going to die. Becoming a nun meant becoming a lady-in-waiting to Mary. But the garden temple of Mary has been destroyed. The grove is gone from the world. Nobody builds sunken gardens anymore. Mary's temple was destroyed by the followers of the Masculine God, the God whose son was Christ, the Conceptual God of Mind and Logos, and so all the ladies-in-waiting to Mary wander about the world lost without temple or shrine. When my life of painting was taken from me the temple was torn down again. The temple of the rose is always being torn down. Mary loves the rose. Oh yes, She loves the rose."

It started to rain. I went into the house and left Tante Huguette alone in the garden. I went to my study and took a book down from the shelf and looked out the window at the rain dripping through the leaves of the linden. I flipped through the book to a reproduction of Filippo Lippi's *Annunciation* and looked deep into the eyes of Mary, the Mary who Filippo Lippi took into his bed in Venice. What kind of Mary would go to bed with an artist like that? Whatever became of the children born to him and his beautiful madonna Lucrezia Buti?

Chapter 11

Day 2:
The Children of Filippo
Lippi and Lucrezia Buti

> "All this gossip surrounding the life of
> [Filippo Lippi] for a long time prevented
> any more objective approach to his
> works, which today are finally
> recognized as being among the most
> original and important examples of
> Italian Quattrocento art."
> *Filippo Lippi*, The Library of Great
> Masters, Gloria Fossi.

"After Filippo Lippi kidnapped Lucrezia Buti from her convent, they had two children together", I said, "a boy and a girl. They didn't live in Venice however, as I said yesterday, but in the town of Prato where Lucrezia Buti had been a nun at the convent of Santa Margherita. Their son followed in his father's footsteps and became a renowned painter, but nothing is really known of the daughter."

I was reading to Tante Huguette from the book I had found in my study. We were in the garden. We were getting along much better after our explosive outburst of the day before. We had calmed down. We had cleared the air. She was still wearing her rosary of sorrow but the images of Mary carved in each bead looked softer as if washed by a storm, or by tears, or by a storm of tears.

"I would like to think that the daughter of Lucrezia Buti had her mother's eyes." Tante Huguette said. "They are the eyes of the Magdelaine."

I said: "If Lucrezia Buti's daughter had her mother's eyes, where would she go when it was time to consecrate her life to Mary Magdelaine? I mean, she would certainly want to consecrate herself to the Magdelaine if she was seeing the world through Her eyes. But then, if the Magdelaine has been rejected for two thousand years, wouldn't that woman's inner Magdelaine be rejected over and over in her life? I've been thinking about this all night. I've been thinking endlessly about everything you said yesterday."

Tante Huguette said: "And I have been shedding tears all night, tears for my darling Claudette, who was like my own daughter, and who

I expected to live the life I never lived, to finish all the paintings I couldn't finish because I died so young. I will feel sad about Claudette forever. And I will feel sad about myself, because I don't know who I am without her."

"Your suffering is over." I said. "Claudette has set you free. She has taken all the sorrow you gave her and put it into her new paintings in Montreal. You are free to return home, to your real home. You see, I think I know who you are and where you come from. I have evolved a whole theory about you overnight. It is quite extensive really. Look at this. It is a photograph of a wood carving by Donatello, done in 1454[1] near the end of his life. My theory about you begins with this carving: I believe that this carving is a portrait of Lucrezia Buti's daughter. According to the dates alone it is possible. It is possible that Donatello knew Filippo Lippi's daughter and that he did a sculpture of her. And look: she looks exactly like you."

"Oh my God!" she said. "Do I look like that! Just look at me! Look at those eyes!"

Donatello's carving *Mary Magdelaine*, (poplar wood, 1454), shows a haggard and wasted old woman with ravaged features and sunken eyes. She looks like someone who has been wandering the hills and lonely places of the Earth forever. The slim, knotted wood of the poplar is perfectly suited for this carving.

Tante Huguette touched her own face then touched the face of Donatello's *Mary Magdelaine* in the photograph. "My eyes." she said. "Yes, those are my eyes."

Then she pushed the book away and began weeping great tears that dropped like rain from the boughs of a linden. The linden is also a good wood for carving. It is not exactly a "modern" wood, but it is associated more with North American sculpture than with that of Europe. The statue of Margeurite Bourgeoys in the church of Notre Dame de Bon Secours in Montreal is carved from a linden. Tante Huguette loved that carving, and this love led her to a love for all linden trees, especially for how they move in the wind, in the fierce wind that comes in night storms. Most wood carvings of Renaissance Italy, on the other hand, like the carving of *Our Lady of Perugia*, are done in poplar.

Tante Huguette recognized herself immediately in Donatello's carving, and she knew right away that she was the lost daughter of Filippo Lippi and Lucrezia Buti.

---

[1] Janson's *History of Art*, p 483.

Personally, I had thought that this was a radical supposition, and I had developed a whole theory overnight to support it. The first part of the theory was that the carving by Donatello was done after Lucrezia Buti's daughter had spent years wandering Italy looking for a sacred place where she could consecrate herself to the Magdelaine. The carving was done at the exact moment when Lucrezia Buti's daughter realized that there was not one temple to Mary Magdelaine left anywhere in the world.

In my research I had found that in Italy in early Christian times there had been cathedrals and churches named for Mary Magdelaine and Orders of nuns dedicated to Her. This was a key part of my theory. I suggested that although no system of worship to the Magdelaine existed anymore in the 15th Century, Filippo Lippi and Lucrezia Buti had unknowingly, or unconsciously, followed the forgotten rites of one of these disbanded Orders of nuns.

There was, for instance, an Order of nuns called the *Holy Sisters of Mary Magdelaine* instituted under the patronage of Pope Julius II in Rome, and continued under Leo X and Clement VII. The convent of *the Holy Order of Mary Magdelaine* was supported by the earnings of a sacred brothel. It is believed that the prostitutes and the nuns were one and the same women. Pope Innocent III, referring to another collegia of sacred prostitutes, proclaimed that any man who married one of them received a special blessing in heaven. (Encycl.Brit. *prostitution*)

I had also found that there was a strong likelihood that joint Orders of monks and nuns existed who were dedicated to enacting 'the sacred marriage'. This idea was based on a fragment I found in *The Woman's Encyl. of Myths & Secrets* about a dual cathedral in 12th Century Milan which was named for both Mary Magdelaine and John the Evangelist who were believed, by some, to have married after Christ's death. The cathedral was run jointly by monks of St John and nuns of Mary Magdelaine.

My theory concluded with two points: One; Filippo Lippi and Lucrezia Buti made their deep dedication to Mary Magdelaine simply by honouring what was passionate in themselves, by loving what was fruitful in each other, and by trusting the sacredness of physical love. Two; this is the kind of nun that Tante Huguette wanted to be, but like the lost daughter of Filippo Lippi and Lucrezia Buti, she had nowhere to go to consecrate her life to this Mary.

That is what I had planned to say. And there were other things that I had planned to say to Tante Huguette, but she wouldn't stop crying. I had wanted to tell her about another theory of mine that I had been evolving since 1971 when I stood in front of the carving of *Our Lady of*

Perugia in the National Gallery of Umbria and saw the statue of Our Lady move. My theory was about the particular poplar tree from which that statue was carved. This is my theory: that poplar tree must have stood on the top of a hill overlooking the triangle of Assisi, Perugia, and Siena. In the middle of the afternoon, in the middle of summer, in the middle of the fourteenth Century, a man and a woman walked up that hill and stood beside that poplar tree and tried to see as far as the distant blue of the Mediterranean Sea. What happened next happened very, very slowly - as slowly as the sun moves across the sky, as slowly as the shadow of the poplar moves across the grass: everything became still. And in that moment of stillness the artist who carved *Our Lady of Perugia* was conceived.

To be precise, he was conceived in the exact moment when the stillness ended and the shade of the poplar moved suddenly and exposed the man and the woman to the blue of the sky. "Will our love last forever?" the woman had asked. "Oh yes, forever." the man had answered. Then, suddenly, the stillness ended and a mysterious wind blew in from the sea and the woman opened her eyes and looked deep into the eyes of the man, and in that exact moment the poplar tree swayed suddenly in the mysterious wind, and the woman's eyes were filled with blue. They were filled with the blue of the sky, and they were filled with the blue of the sea that reflected the blue of the sky. Now the man was inside her, and the mysterious wind was inside her, and the colour blue was inside her. And that was my whole story. That was as far as I got in my theory of why the artist gave *Our Lady of Perugia* blue eyes.

I wanted to ask Tante Huguette what she knew about the mysterious wind. I stood there watching her cry. I wanted her to speak to me and tell me that the mysterious wind was the same wind that had entered Fra Filippo Lippi's paintings in Prado and had blown like Gabriel through his heart until he had stirred the heart of Mary and had taken her out of the painting and into his bed. I wanted to know if this same wind had stirred my own heart in Perugia when I saw the statue of Our Lady move. I wanted to know if this stirring in my heart had stirred the heart of Our Lady and reminded Her that She was a poplar tree, and that She had stood on the top of a hill looking across the Umbrian Plain toward the Mediterranean Sea, and that She had been stirred by a mysterious breeze. I wanted to know if all statues made from poplars are moved by the same breeze? Is this the breeze that entered Persian poetry in the thirteenth century with the birth of Rumi? Is the breeze in me?

I didn't have this talk with Tante Huguette. She wept for a long time in the walled garden. She wept for the dark beauty she saw in her own eyes, in the eyes of Donatello's carving *Mary Magdelaine*. I started to imagine that she was weeping for my theories, for the need to make them up in the first place when the answers were all in my heart. The next day I learned the truth: she was weeping because Donatello understood her, and because I understood her.

"No man has understood me before." She said. "Do you think Augustine Baker will understand me?" This is what she needed to know the next day. But when we were in the garden and I was watching her weep, I said: "I must talk to you about something. Two nights ago, as I made love to Claudette, she held me tight and said my name three times. As she did this I imagined myself standing at the edge of a sacred grove, where eyes like yours looked out at me from inside the grove, and they said that I could not go further because a secret was kept there, and they said that if I went further I must die. Well, tell me, what do I have to do to die? How do I get to the heart of matter where the secret is?"

I didn't actually say this to Tante Huguette. In fact, we didn't speak again that day after I showed her the picture of the carving by Donatello. She wept and I watched her. Occasionally she would look up and look around the garden. The sun came out and went back in. A soft breeze picked up and blew gently through the linden. Was the breeze from Persia? Or was the breeze Gabriel? Was Mary swaying in the linden?

Chapter 12:
The Third Day

> "The messenger-angel Gabriel, who
> brought the Divine Message to the
> prophet [Mohammed], is also the
> archangel who breathed the Divine
> spirit into Mary's womb."
> *The Celestial Garden*,
> Anne Marie Schimmel.

Tante Huguette came into the garden the next day wearing a long robe of the deepest blue. It completely covered her body. She looked like a fifteenth century Italian sky. Her eyes were the eyes of Lucrezia Buti. I said that I was ready to die, and she said that she was ready to discuss marriage. She added that she would never, ever, marry Augustine Baker. "You will have to find someone else for me." she said. "I am gravely concerned that in everything you have told me about Augustine Baker, he has shown no devotion to Mary or to the rosary."

"You can relax." I said. "Augustine Baker has a direct and concrete connection with the history of the rosary. You see, the Benedictine Chapter House to which he belonged was the English Benedictine monastery-in-exile in the town of Douai in Alsace. Two hundred years before Baker's time, right there in Douai, the first confraternity of the rosary was started. It was started by a french Black Friar named Alain de la Roche. It seems that de la Roche tried to legitimize the rosary as a form of Marian devotion by attributing its discovery to Saint Dominic. He claimed that Dominic was given the first rosary by Mary Herself in a profound vision in which Mary suckled Dominic at Her breast and then presented him with the prayer beads as a means of repeating this intimacy with Her endlessly.

"However, this form of erotic mysticism was judged to be more typical of Alain de la Roche than of St Dominic. De la Roche, you see, was considered slightly mad, and the application to the Papacy for the recognition of the Douai confraternity of the rosary was rejected. The first confraternity to be officially recognized was at Cologne in 1475."

Tante Huguette said: "Now I feel much better." She was smiling. "You know, I think I prefer Alain de la Roche to Augustine Baker."

"Not so fast." I said. "Although Augustine Baker did not have a deep devotion to the rosary, he had a deep devotion to language which is just as good because the history of language and the history of the rosary are intrinsically connected.

"You see, the essential form of the rosary is nothing other than knot-writing, and if you look at the Sanskrit word for knot, *granthi*, you will see that by extension it also means 'an artificial pattern of words'. Similarly in Sanskrit, *sutra* means both 'a spun thread' and 'a sacred book'."

I went on to explain that the purpose of the rosary is to bring the user to a state of continual 'recollection'. The term was first fully articulated in the Christian tradition by Cassian, although the method of recollection he recommended was not the rosary but the mantra. The rosary did not appear in the West until eight centuries after Cassian's death. In fact, the counting of prayers on beads did not enter Western Culture in any significant way until the Crusades. Mary did not enter the complex until the 11th Century, and it was not until the 15th Century that the term rosarium became current and Papal approval was granted for the praying to Mary on the five-decade beads. Before that time beads strung together in varying numbers were usually known as pater-noster beads.

"Tell me," Tante Huguette said, "is your Augustine Baker as clever with language as you?"

"Language is just a rosary." I said. "Writing is the stringing together of knots, and reading is the mumbling we do over them. Language is simply another form of recollection. We honestly expect the threaded knots of our words to tell us who we are, (who we are *already* and *always* in our eternal selves), and we expect these threaded knots to lead us home, to lead us out of this prison of speech and off of this walled page forever! Language is a spiritual practice. We read from left to right and go from word to word feeling the strength of the thread and the quality of the weave, but we are looking for something more. We are looking for what the knots create when they are strung together, we are looking for the perfect word, or the perfect pattern of words, that will tell us who we are beyond all our appearances. You see, yesterday in the garden I realized that I long for death, that I long for the reality that underlies language.

"All my life I have gone from page to page looking for it, from book to book, around and around the beads of my rosary heart. I don't want to go around like this forever. But how I love to do it! I am ready to die and find the meaning at the heart of language."

Tante Huguette nodded her head slowly. She was quiet a long time. Then she took a deep, considered breath and held it. Then she let out her breath in a great long sigh full of sadness and understanding and patient, patient, grace.

"Yes, yes. I agree to the proposal of your Augustine Baker. Yes, I shall be his bride."

Then Tante Huguette shook her head and laughed: "Language had to be a gift from the angels", she said, "because only you angels can yearn this way. You yearn for paradise, for the real paradise beyond appearance. Well, perhaps if you had sucked better at your mother's breast you would not yearn so badly. Yes, I understand your frustration now in trying to fall to Earth: you are afraid to become as mad as Alain de la Roche and to learn to suck endlessly from the breast of the Lady you love. And yet you must become like him and let go of your pious hold on language, your fervent devotion to "meaning". It is time now to restore paradise to Her, to Lady Magdelaine, the one you love. I agree to marry your Augustine Baker. Together we can rebuild the temple of the true Mary, and restore Her place in the hearts of men.

"Come closer", she said, "and let me show you the secret I have kept hidden from you beneath my robe. Come closer and see what has been kept from you all these years."

The shadows were growing long across the garden and the light was beginning to fade. It was coming on eventide of the third day. Tante Huguette was beginning to open her deep blue robe to show me the secret that she kept there, the secret that required me to die to my old life and forsake my ability to hover at a theoretical height above myself where the complicated pattern of my life fell into perfect order and symmetry. Everything is beautiful from there. You can see as far as the Euphrates River and the borders of Ancient Egypt. I will always love the view from the tops of hills. I can stand there for hours and take photographs, then put them in my study and look at them and remember.

Tante Huguette opened her robe a little more and I felt a great pain in my back, as if the last of my wings were being torn from between my shoulder blades. The light that had been shining on me - the light that had been shining down the axis from heaven, the light that was Augustine Baker's presence in my life - moved all the way down through my body and into the Earth. And I felt roots growing rapidly downward from my feet anchoring me against my upward tendency.

"Stop this!" I said. "Stop it! I will be trapped here forever!" Tante Huguette, who had become the Lady of the Rose entirely, smiled and opened her deep blue robe all the way. In her arms she held a little child, a baby girl.

"This is the child born of the Magdelaine." she said. "You have been looking for her a long time. She is the one who brings new life into the world and the Magdelaine has protected her since her birth long ago. She is the one to whom you must make your Annunciation, oh Gabriel."

I went down on one knee and placed my right hand over my heart. I looked at the child in Tante Huguette's arms. Then I looked up at Tante Huguette and her face was the face of Our Lady of Perugia. Her missing arm had been restored and in it she carried the child. The child's eyes were as blue as the sky and the sea. Her eyes were looking into the blue of Our Lady's blue eyes, and Our Lady's blue eyes were looking at me. '

So often in paintings of *the Annunciation* the Lady is shown holding a book. Fra Angelico himself shows Her this way in his second fresco of *The Annunciation* at San Marco. I thought for sure that when I saw the Lady of Perugia again, and saw Her missing arm restored, and saw Her arms reaching out to hold me, that She would be carrying a book. I had often imagined myself glancing discretely at that book during our tender loving embrace. I imagined myself barely glimpsing the text but still catching its meaning, knowing that this meaning was the meaning that is hidden beneath all text. I imagined myself remembering the meaning and writing it down later.

But now that I have seen what Our Lady carries under the blue of Her deep blue cape, how can I find words to describe the beauty on the face of the child and the meaning in the blue of those blue, blue eyes. I was looking into the eyes of the lost daughter of Mary Magdelaine and her lover, Jesus Christ.

That's when I died. I died when I looked into the eyes of the baby girl and saw the passion of Christ and the passion of the Magdelaine meeting each other. That was exactly the kind of love I had experienced for a brief moment with the Lady of the Rose in Her sacred grove when I was making love to Claudette, the kind of love I thought I would never feel again in the world. And that's when I died - right then. I died from longing, and I died from a broken heart.

Epilogue I
A Note on the Rosary

> "... Mary [Magdelaine] stood weeping
> outside the tomb... she turned around
> and saw Jesus standing, but she did not
> know that it was Jesus. Jesus said to
> her, "Woman, why are you weeping?
> Whom do you seek?" Supposing him to
> be the gardener, she said to him, "Sir, if
> you have carried him away, tell me
> where you have laid him, and I will take
> him away."
> *John 20:11.*

I have always loved the rosary and its circular counting in end-less repetition. It is a form of narrative like the continuous prose of the novel.

In the moment of my death when I looked into the blue of the baby girl's blue eyes, I found myself wondering: who was the first person who tied a series of knots in a length of thread and then joined the ends of the thread together so that the thread became infinite and each knot became a word? How did this person explain to the world that when you touch a knot your attention is taken a way from the knot to something else entirely? How do you explain it - that when you touch one of the knots you feel the meaning that's hidden in the word?

Our prayers are endless.

When I died I did not die physically of course, but I died to my old way of living, to my old habit of hovering above myself. I like to think that in the moment of my death I became more like Alain de la Roche; that is, I found myself evolving a whole new theory about how the rosary came into the hands of human beings. This is my theory: the rosary wasn't given to us by the angels, or by God, it was given to us by a baby girl who was sitting in the lap of a Lady for two thousand years. And she didn't give the rosary to Saint Dominic, she gave it to me.

I learned many things in the moment of my death, as if I had always known them and was simply remembering them for the first time. For instance, I learned that this moment - this moment right now, (which for you is the moment of reading these words) - is the same as the moment of my death. I learned that every moment is really the same moment. Therefore, if the moment of my death is like any moment, then this moment of reading is the same as the moment of dying.

Nothing really changed when I died, except that I no longer held my place of overview from which I could see myself within the vast expanse of history, and that I began experiencing history in the very moment of my awareness of myself. Let me clarify this point by giving you an example: in the moment of my death I realized, (realized in a feeling way), that the moment of my death was identical to the moment in 1678 when the priest held his hands together and raised the chalice of wine high above his head during the first Mass ever celebrated at the Church of Notre Dame de Bon Secours in Montreal, (then called Ville-Marie), and in particular, my death was like the brief moment of pause when the chalice was held at the furthest extension of the priest's arms and everything became still; and the moment of my death was like the moment four hundred years before the moment in Ville-Marie when, at the new cathedral in Chartres, the glaziers climbed down from the scaffolds and stood back and saw the rose window complete for the first time; like the moment seven hundred years later when my father's heart beat for the last time; or the moment when you turned a page of this book, then turned back the page, the moment when you held the page between your thumb and forefinger, and paused, just like the priest paused in Ville-Marie in 1678; like the moment when the pause ended and you went on reading; like the moment when there are no pages to turn anymore and your own heart beats for the last time.

Every moment is this moment.

I saw all this in the blueness of the baby girl's blue eyes. And there is something else I saw in her eyes, something that taught me how to die and helped me to stop hovering above myself and which completed my fall to Earth.

When I went down on one knee in front of the baby girl and looked in her eyes, she held out her arms to me as if she wanted me to hold her, and in her little hand, in the tiny fingers of her hand, she held a rosary. I looked at the rosary, then I looked in her eyes, and her eyes said everything:

her eyes said that each bead of the rosary
was a human heart.
And her eyes said that the string joining
the beads together is the tunnel or axis that passes
through the centre of the novel, the axis that
I experienced passing through my own heart, the axis that
goes from Heaven down to the centre of the Earth.
And her eyes said that each of us has

this axis passing through us
and that
we are all strung together on this string.
The eyes of the baby girl said that
as human beings we are each a part of the rosary,
and that we are strung together at the heart,
and that each heart is a prayer on the lips of a baby girl
who sits in the lap of a Lady.

This was all communicated to me in a moment. I looked at the eyes of the baby girl, and I looked at the rosary in her hand, and I knew that each bead of the rosary was a human life and was also, at the same time, one single beat in the continuous beating of my heart. I also knew that the baby girl was a symbol for new life and possibility that was entering the world.

So tell me, if the baby girl is a symbol for new life and possibility, is the new life growing out of the depth in you too? And if this new life is growing out of the depth in you, then tell me, does it feel the same as something that grows from the Earth and reaches for the sun?

For my part, I experienced it as a light shining down through me and reaching into the depth of the Earth. And when I looked into the eyes of the baby girl I knew that I was the anchor for this light in the world, and that my love of the girl anchored it, and that the light was anchored in my heart. But that's not my point. I need to know if you understand my relationship to the baby girl. I mean, in your own opinion, when she reached out her arms to me in the moment when our eyes met (in the moment when I came to Earth completely and she reached out her arms to me as if she wanted me to pick her up), can you tell me whether she was reaching for the light of the sun that was anchored in my heart, or was she reaching to be held in the arms of her father?

Epilogue II
A Note on The Colour Blue

> "... [The lord's] clothes were full and
> flowing and seemly. Their colour was
> the blue of the sky, restrained but
> beautiful. The lord was sitting in
> solemn state, and his servant standing
> reverently behind him. [I wondered]
> what sort of work the servant had to do.
> Then I understood: he was off to do
> work that was the hardest and most
> exhausting possible. He was to be a
> gardener..."
> *Revelations of Divine Love*,
> Julian of Norwich.

In the Greek language blue is the most beautiful colour: it is the colour of the sky and the colour of the sea and the colour of the eyes of Pallas Athene. In the Hebrew language there is no word for blue: the closest word to blue in the Old Testament is 'takleth', the word for a bluish-purple dye obtained from the shellfish murex which is used in wool and other fabrics. It is the blue in hand-woven carpets.

When Christianity took the biblical commentaries of the Alexandrian Hebrew scholar Philo and made his allegorical interpretation of the Bible its framework for identifying Christ's significance in the universe, (identifying Christ as Logos - the impersonal principle which provides order and intelligibility to the universe), Christianity took as its inheritance both the literal faith of the Hebrews and the conceptual abstraction of the Greeks. The Hebrews gave Christianity its sacred book, and the Greeks provided the framework within which to understand the text. Indeed, the true value of having a Greek commentary on the Bible is that it showed us the significance of the margin for the first time: the text is the place of the literal sense, and the margin is the wall around it from which the meaning can be seen. However, this linguistic framework, this schematic outline of the universe, leaves the light of Christ out on the margin, and leaves us humans inside the text tying knots and stringing them together in endless prayers of perfect longing for the light. The mystics among us are those who have insisted that there is no distinction between the margin and the text. But they have always told us this in a linguistic system founded on the separation.

Let me put it more simply: when the mystics struggled with language they were trying to demonstrate how we can all be on the margin and in the text at the same time, how we can be in the garden and on the wall in the same moment, and how we can bring Heaven and Earth together by letting the light and the dark stand together in our hearts.

Let me give you an example: The carpet in the antechamber to my bedroom is blue. The blue is from the shellfish murex. The carpet was woven in Iran in the particular style of the Tabriz area. This is the carpet whose pattern I had copied ten years earlier when I drew a design for the walled garden. It is also the carpet on which I made love to Claudette on the night she stayed at my house and we sat in the kitchen talking until midnight drinking two bottles of wine. Claudette came back to visit me the following October. She came to see the changes I had made to the garden, and she came as part of our plan to sit down together and discuss the future of our relationship. I'll never forget the moment she came walking through the gate into the backyard. I was sitting on the love seat in the shaded grove waiting for her. Then I heard the latch of the gate open. I stood up and waited for the latch to close again. Then I heard what I was waiting for, I heard Claudette's voice calling my name loudly from the other end of the yard. I stepped from behind the lattice divider and saw her standing by the gate with her hands to her mouth staring at the new sunken garden and at the ring of trees surrounding it. I had spent months tranforming the garden, and Claudette looked astonished. I must have looked astonished too, because when I looked at Claudette I saw that she was seven months pregnant.

Claudette has blue eyes. Our daughter has blue eyes. Our daughter is now ten years old. Claudette became pregnant on the night I made love to her on the blue Tabriz carpet in front of the fireplace in the antechamber to the bedroom.

Before I learned that Claudette was pregnant the plan had been for her to visit my new garden and to stay long enough so that we could talk about the future of our relationship. Then, no matter what we decided about our marriage, we would go back to Montreal together to celebrate the elevation to sainthood of Margeurite Bourgeoys, the founder of the order of nuns in which Tante Huguette had been a novice. You see, Margeurite Bourgeoys had been canonized by Pope John Paul II on April 2, 1982. Coincidentally, this was the same day on which Tante Huguette accepted the marriage proposal of Augustine Baker in the walled garden at the back of my house. The Feast Day for Margeurite Bourgeoys was to be November 1, All Saints Day. A celebration was planned in Montreal for the eve of All Saints, and we wanted to be there for that. We wouldn't miss it for anything.

I showed Claudette all the changes I had made to the garden. I told her that I had done all the work myself - which was almost true - I had hired someone to excavate the hole in the ground for the sunken garden, and then I had done all the stonework myself.

I handled each stone with both hands and lifted them into place one at a time. There are five courses of rough stone and a capping course of chiseled Owen Sound stone. The sunken garden is in the shape of a modified *mihrab*, or prayer arch, which is often the central medallion in Persian carpets. Then, around the sunken garden, I planted a ring of trees.

When Claudette entered the garden and saw the ring of trees and the sunken garden she looked astonished. She said: "It's the 'Sacred Grove of the Mothers'. How could you know what it looks like. Your garden looks exactly like the grove of the Mothers, the place deep inside myself where I went during my year of Sorrow. How could you know? How is this possible!?"

I couldn't take my eyes off Claudette's belly. I was about to say to Claudette: "I didn't know until just now that it was the grove of the Mothers," (I was intending this to be a joke that would cover up my profound awkwardness in the moment,) but before I could speak Claudette walked closer to the sunken garden and said: "No, I'm wrong, it can't be the grove of the Mothers."

Immediately I knew that she was referring to the fact that I had used pyramidal oaks rather than poplars and laurels to ring the sunken garden, even though Tante Huguette's plan had called for poplars and laurels specifically. I said: "The pyramidal oak is much more appropriate for the Canadian climate. The leaves turn a copper colour in Fall and remain on the tree in winter. I did everything else exactly as outlined by Tante Huguette in her list of design requirements. You see, the marriage between her and Augustine Baker could not take place until the garden was finished. There had to be a sacred grove first, a temple to the Magdelaine, the true Lady of the Rose."

Claudette said, "That's not what I mean." She inclined her head to one side slightly, nodding toward the centre of the grove. I looked in the direction she indicated and saw that she was pointing to Tante Huguette and Augustine Baker who were sitting at the centre of the sunken garden. They were sitting quietly with their hands in their laps. Claudette said that she had never known a man to be in the grove before.

Tante Huguette looked like the Lady of the Rose. She was wearing a simple dress of white, and upon her head she wore a crown of laurels. Augustine Baker was wearing a long robe of a distinguished tone of dark blue, and under the robe he was wearing my father's sky-blue tunic. Then Augustine Baker stood up and turned to us and announced in a solemn voice that he and Tante Huguette had decided to marry the next night. "Not tonight," he said, "tomorrow night, the eve of All Saints Day. You both must be there — that is, all three of you must be there."

Claudette and I looked at each other, then Claudette took my arm and we walked to the back porch. Claudette said: "Tell me what's been happening here. Exactly. Tell me everything." We stopped for a moment on the porch then walked into the house. Augustine Baker and Tante Huguette didn't move all that day or all the next day. They sat completely still with utter patience. They could have been figures in a sixteenth century Persian garden painting, like the illustration to the text of *Babur-Nama*, the autobiography of the Persian ruler who built the garden *Bagh-i-Wafa* at Kabul. They were the lovers who embrace secretly inside the diamond-shaped medallion at the centre of Persian carpets.

Claudette and I didn't go to Montreal after all. We wanted to stay and witness the marriage of Augustine Baker and the Lady of the Rose. So, we went into the house and started talking, and we talked all day long and we talked into the night. Then we talked all the next day too. And by the time night came to the garden we had told each other everything - all our secrets, and all our hopes and fears and plans and regrets - and then the moon rose in the night sky and Augustine Baker and Tante Huguette stood up together at the centre of the sunken garden and looked at each other. Augustine Baker presented Tante Huguette with a single rose, and upon the rose was a single drop of dew. Claudette and I watched from the edge of the sunken garden. We were ready to witness everything that was about to occur on this holy night. We expected the night to be amazing and startling and maybe transforming.

But then, just as Tante Huguette and Augustine Baker were about to exchange their vows, they turned to us and invited us to come and stand with them at the centre of the grove, and when we joined them they disappeared and Claudette and I were left standing alone in the sunken garden under the vast autumn night sky. Claudette was moving her lips silently repeating over and over the phrase Maranatha, the prayer of the Lady in Black who was Elizabeth Fortesque, the prayer of the Lady of the Rose who saved my life when I was ten, the prayer of all the Ladies who had been waiting patiently from century to century for this moment.

I stood alone with Claudette at the centre of the sunken garden. The night grew dark around us. A gentle breeze began to stir the leaves of the pyramidal oaks surrounding us, and then the leaves on the ground began to blow and tumble across the yard, and smoke from a neighbour's fire drifted through the grove towards us. Claudette shivered in the chill air and I put an arm around her.

The wind died down and I looked up at the moon and saw my breath against the stars.

It was a beautiful autumn night, and all was calm and all was still. This is not what I expected. I kept looking up to the stars and then looking around the yard. I expected the heavens to open and all the saints to array themselves in gold vestments row upon row in tiers on the garden wall, singing and raising their arms in celebration of the wedding and of the elevation to sainthood of Margeurite Bourgeoys. This was the night of the Assumption and the Descent, the night when Mary Magdelaine would be assumed out of the darkest part of the dark into the light of the grove and her lover would return to take his place beside her in paradise.

Instead, everything was quiet as if the sacred grove was just a metaphor for my heart, as if the image of assumption and descent was just an extension of that metaphor, as if heaven did not exist and the dark did not exist, as if my daughter was a literary image representing an abstract concept that stood for the new life of the world that is born whenever someone opens their heart to the sacred marriage of the masculine and feminine inside themselves, as if the ladies-in-waiting to Mary Magdelaine and the canon of saints from heaven had never intended to make separate processions into the walled garden and form a joint circle around the grove and sing in harmony like an ancient community of monks and nuns in the processional song at Vespers.

That is what I imagined would happen. And I imagined that Augustine Baker would lead the procession of the saints and that Tante Huguette would lead the procession of the ladies-in-waiting who had been wandering the world for centuries without temple or shrine, one procession coming down from the light and the other arising from the dark, the two lines swirling together and joining around the sunken garden, voices quivering and trembling on the night air, candles winking like starlight, the circle growing tighter and voices growing like thunder that rolls across the sky and shudders the windows of a house and rattles the family heirlooms in the display case against the dining room wall.

This was the night when the lost temple of the Magdelaine returned to the world from the darkest part of the dark and became the grove of the lovers and the temple of the sacred marriage. This was the night when the text and the margin swirled together and merged, the night when the gardener and the landscape architect embraced, the night when old hurts were forgiven and all differences reconciled. But nothing happened. I kept expecting that if Tante Huguette and Augustine Baker were not coming back to lead their processions to the sacred grove, they should at least come back so that Tante Huguette, as a lady-in-waiting to the Lady of the Rose, could turn to Claudette and place on her head the crown of laurels, and Augustine Baker could reach into the pocket of my father's tunic and take from it my father's good luck charm and flip it to me casually, winking and saying: "That's the other half of your father's half-crown: one half from the father and the other half from the great father", smiling and placing a hand nonchalantly in his trouser pocket and winking again like I think I remember my father winking, or like I imagine he must have winked at friends or the men in his squadron or at his own son when he said good-bye to him for the last time. But nothing like that happened. Claudette and I just stood there alone at the centre of the universe. All was calm and all was still. The whole garden was held in the stillness. Claudette and I stood there a long time while the moon moved in its course across the quiet night sky, and then we smiled at each other and shook our heads, and then I bent down and put my ear to her belly and I listened while Claudette put her right hand on the crown of my head and I told her that the stillness of the night and the stillness of the universe was right inside her. "No really," I said, "It's right here." And we both laughed, but it was true, I could hear the stillness of the night and the stillness of the universe in each beat of our daughter's beating heart.